SAMURAI KIDS

SHAOLIN TIGER

SAMURAI KIDS

SHAOLIN TIGER

SANDY FUSSELL

CANDLEWICK PRESS

Text copyright © 2009 by Sandy Fussell
Illustrations copyright © 2009 by Rhian Nest James

First U.S. edition 2011

Library of Congress Cataloging-in-Publication Data

Fussell, Sandy.
Shaolin tiger / Sandy Fussell ; [illustrations by Rhian Nest James].
— 1st U.S. ed.
p.   cm. — (Samurai kids ; [3])
Summary: Sensei Ki-Yaga leads the disabled samurai-in-training of the Cockroach Ryu across the Sea of Japan to China, where they study the ways of the Shaolin monks before facing Qing-Shen, a skilled soldier seeking revenge against his former teacher, the Sensei.
ISBN 978-0-7636-5702-4
[1. Samurai — Fiction. 2. People with disabilities — Fiction.
3. Hand-to-hand fighting, Oriental — Fiction. 4. Soldiers — Fiction.
5. Schools — Fiction. 6. Japan — Fiction. 7. China — Fiction.]
I. James, Rhian Nest, date, ill. II. Title. III. Series.
PZ7.F96669Sh 2011
[Fic] — dc22   2010052614

11 12 13 14 15 16 BVG 10 9 8 7 6 5 4 3 2 1

Printed in Berryville, VA, U.S.A.

This book was typeset in Garamond Three.

Candlewick Press
99 Dover Street
Somerville, Massachusetts 02144

visit us at www.candlewick.com

For Neridah, like the tiger, strong in spirit
S. F.

For Lowri Gwenllian
R. N. J.

THE SAMURAI KIDS

KYOKO A girl with white hair, pink eyes, and extra fingers and toes. Her spirit is the Snow Monkey.

MIKKO A boy with one arm. His spirit is the Striped Gecko.

NIYA The boy with one leg who narrates
      the story. His spirit is the White Crane.

YOSHI A huge, strong boy who doesn't want
       to fight. His spirit is the Tiger.

TAJI A boy who is blind. His spirit
is the Golden Bat.

NEZUME The last boy to join the Cockroach Ryu.
His spirit is the Long-Tailed Rat.

THE TEACHER

SENSEI Also known as Ki-Yaga the wizard. He
was once a famous samurai warrior.

CONTENTS

CHAPTER ONE

真

INTO THE OCEAN

Yoshi's voice booms across the deck, through the thick gloom and above the waves pounding against the hull. "Man overboard!"

I look around in panic. There are only two men on this boat; the rest are kids. One of the men is Sensei Ki-Yaga, and the other is the ship's master, Captain Oong.

"Mikko, drop the anchor. Kyoko, bring a long rope from the stern," shouts Sensei.

His orders mean that our teacher is safe, but I'm afraid for the captain. Not even a hardened sailor could survive long in this bad-tempered ocean.

"Fetch the lantern from our quarters," Sensei calls to Taji. "Go quickly."

Some people would think it strange to send a kid who is blind to find something, when every moment spent looking could be the difference between life and death. But Taji is more skilled at finding things in the dark than anyone else. It's what he does every day.

People misjudge us all the time. Mikko, with his one arm, and Taji, who is blind. Yoshi, a samurai kid who refuses to fight. Kyoko, with her bright white hair and her extra fingers and toes. And me, with one leg. Other people think these things make us weak. But we know better: they make us strong.

"I heard a splash here." Yoshi points. "Then I heard Captain Oong cry out for help."

Searching for movement, I peer across the angry waters. I am Niya Moto, the White Crane. By day my eyes can pick the flash of a fish scale from miles above the ocean, but now it's hard to see. The dim moon reveals a landscape of dark shadows. The howling and blustering wind pummels the shadows into grotesque shapes. Monsters rise and fall back into the waves.

Only one shadow isn't changing form.

"I think I see him!" I yell.

My friends crowd around, hopeful.

Kyoko leans precariously over the edge of the boat and gazes into the storm. "I can't see anything."

"Me either," says Mikko.

Taji returns with the lantern, and Sensei lights the oil wick. The gloom reaches out to swallow the pale beam as quickly as it swallowed our captain, but there is still enough light for the White Crane to be certain of what it saw.

"It is him!" I shriek against the wind.

"I'll go," volunteers Yoshi. "I'm the best swimmer."

No one argues. We're all good swimmers, but only Yoshi has a hope of making it through the gigantic waves.

He unhooks his sword from his jacket sash and hands it to me. Then his *wakizashi* dagger. *For safekeeping,* his eyes say. *I want you to have them if I don't return.*

Yoshi is very brave.

"A true samurai doesn't need a sword," I tell him.

It's the first lesson Sensei ever taught us and Yoshi's favorite. But now, with Yoshi standing swordless before me, I understand what it really means. My friend is a great warrior, about to battle the ocean with his bare hands.

He hurriedly strips off his clothing. Sash, jacket, kimono, trousers, and undershirt. Finally, Yoshi is standing in his loincloth. It makes me shiver to look at him. Not because his skin is already prickled with goose bumps but because I am afraid. The ocean is more than cold. Its belly is rumbling and roaring, hungry for human flesh.

Deftly, Kyoko ties the rope around Yoshi's waist.

Six fingers on each hand might make some kids laugh, but Kyoko can bind knots even the storm cannot untie. And it's a good thing, too. Yoshi will need all the help he can get.

He bows low to Sensei. It's a mark of great respect. Sensei doesn't bow in return. He takes Yoshi's hands in his and lowers his forehead to them. It's a mark of even greater respect.

"*Chi, jin, yu,*" Sensei murmurs.

Wisdom, benevolence, and courage. The code of the samurai.

A spike of lightning splits the ocean in two, and without hesitating, Yoshi dives into the breach.

Yesterday, when the storm clouds rushed in from the horizon and the sea rose up to meet the wind, the captain laughed. "The Dragon grows angry," he said.

"What dragon?" asked Kyoko.

"A mighty dragon lives beneath the sea, but it doesn't usually wake this time of year. Something has disturbed it, and now it tosses and turns, unable to rest."

"We probably disturbed it." Yoshi grinned. "Dragons have always found us annoying."

We laughed together, remembering the master

A spike of lightning splits the ocean in two, and without hesitating, Yoshi dives into the breach.

and the students of the Dragon Ryu. Before sailing for China, we visited Toyozawa Castle. The Dragon Master was trying to convince the Emperor to allow a war in our mountains. But we soon put a stop to that.

Now the Dragon hates us more than ever. Enough to make the sea spit and foam. Enough to devour the captain.

As we watch Yoshi gouge his way though the waves, our laughter is long gone. The ocean pushes and shoves but Yoshi is powerful, with arms like thickly rolled rice mats. Slowly, he barrels closer to the captain.

With a sharp gasp, Kyoko grabs my arm as Yoshi's head disappears beneath a crest of white water. Mikko, hand tightening on the rope, is ready to haul our friend back to safety.

"Not yet." Sensei rests his fingers on Mikko's one arm. Mikko lost his other arm to the Dragon Master's cruelty long ago, but his remaining arm is strong and a single heave would bring Yoshi plowing back toward us.

I wish Sensei would take his hand away and let Mikko pull. Then I could breathe properly again. I keep holding my breath until I feel light-headed and the White Crane struggles to fly out to Yoshi.

"Pull!" Yoshi shouts, his voice grappling the wind. "I'm coming in."

I breathe out. Around me I hear a soft sigh as my friends do the same.

Kyoko holds the lantern steady, the beam tracking Yoshi with the captain's body now firmly tucked under his arm.

"Yoshi has rescued Captain Oong," I tell Taji, who is standing beside me. "But I can't see if he is alive or not."

"I can find out for you," Taji says.

"How?" I ask. The White Crane has excellent eyes, and Taji has none.

"Is Captain Oong alive?" he bellows across the ocean.

I should have known. Sensei keeps reminding us you don't need to see to get things done. Like his spirit guide, the Golden Bat, Taji can always find a way through the darkness.

"Yes," Yoshi calls, his voice drawing even closer. "The captain lives."

A few minutes and they'll both be back on board. But sometimes minutes crawl so slowly that even a sea snail could outpace them.

Bending deep into the storm, the mast creaks and groans. Wind roars. Waves peak into huge mountains. Lightning slashes and parries across the sky. But Yoshi is almost broadside. Almost safe.

I'm breathing easily again.

Until Kyoko screams.

CHAPTER TWO

仁

ALL AT SEA

A wave rears above Yoshi and crashes down suddenly. Thunder claps to mark the moment. Light floods the ocean, and Yoshi is gone.

I stop breathing.

"Can you see him?" Kyoko tugs at my sleeve.

Frantically, I shake my head.

"Do not be afraid," Sensei says. "I have always taught my students to swim against the tide. We do not need to pull Yoshi back yet."

"It's a very strong tide." Kyoko isn't reassured at all.

Neither am I.

"Yoshi is strong, too," Taji reminds us. "The Tiger is an excellent swimmer."

Unruffled, Taji and Sensei sit in the calm eye of the storm, drawing the rest of us toward them.

Om-om, their chant rises against the gale. *"Om-om,"* I echo. Other voices join in. I feel numb. Disconnected. The White Crane soars above the ocean, searching.

Lightning rips the sky to ribbons, and the rain funnels through. It's even harder to see now.

"Look!" Mikko yells.

It's Yoshi. He raises his hand before diving beneath the foam.

Kyoko panics, pulling at my sleeve again. "What's he doing? Where's the captain?"

"The sea has taken him," I say. "The wave tore the captain from Yoshi's grasp."

"No one could find the captain now. Not even Yoshi." Mikko's voice is strained and anxious.

The ocean surges, shaking its watery fists in triumph.

I sense Yoshi's frustration. My chest tightens. He'll never return to us if he can't bring the captain with him.

Again and again, Yoshi's head bobs above the brine.

"Come in!" bellows Mikko.

"Come back!" Taji calls.

"Please," whispers Kyoko, wiping the rain and tears from her face.

Only the wind answers, a roaring shout of defiance. The Dragon will never be on our side.

"Can we haul him in now, Sensei?" I plead. "The captain is gone, and if we don't act now, we might lose Yoshi, too."

"Yes," our master agrees. "This storm is not content with one body. It is hungry enough to swallow us all. Pull hard, Mikko."

Straining, Mikko heaves against the rope.

"Nooo!" Yoshi howls.

Mikko doesn't stop pulling. I add my strength to his. Taji, Kyoko, and even Sensei pull, too. It should be easy to reel Yoshi back. But now he wrestles against the ocean *and* the tug of the rope.

"No!" Yoshi yells. "I am not ready!"

But we are, and we keep pulling until he touches against the boat.

Kyoko drops a rope ladder over the side. Exhausted, Yoshi clings like a limpet to the rungs.

"Come on, Yosh," I call. "Climb up. You can do it."

Yoshi leans his head into his arms, sobbing against the rope.

"I'll get him." Clambering over the side, Kyoko slides down the wet, slippery ladder. Even the White Crane cannot hear what she whispers, but slowly Yoshi begins to move upward.

Whenever we climb, Yoshi always goes last. Our safety net, waiting to catch us if we fall. But this time Kyoko waits below him. Something has shifted. Something important. The White Crane can feel it in its feathers.

"We need blankets," Sensei says.

"I'll get them," Taji calls, already halfway to our cabin.

As soon as I can reach down to Yoshi, I take his hand. Mikko helps and together we haul our friend on board.

Not even three blankets can stop his shivering.

"The captain is dead. It's all my fault." Yoshi's great shoulders shake like a bough of cherry blossoms in the wind. The flowers fall, and his heart is stripped as bare as the branch. "I let him go," Yoshi moans.

"You did not," I say. "The storm tore his body from you."

"You tried your best," says Taji. "It is all anyone can do. And it was much more than the rest of us put together."

It's hard to know what to say. Yoshi is our rock. But a river of water can wear even a rock down, and tears are flooding down Yoshi's face.

Kyoko wraps her arms around him and holds tight until his sobbing finally stops. A hug from a samurai girl is warmer than a heap of blankets and more meaningful than a pile of words.

"It made no difference," he mumbles into Kyoko's arms. "Trying doesn't mean anything."

"Yes, it does," I insist. "It means everything. What about the day the earthquake rolled me off the side of our mountain? If you didn't try to rescue me then, I wouldn't be here today."

Yoshi says nothing. Life is all about balance. Since I have only one leg, I understand that well. When Yoshi was much younger, he accidentally killed a friend in a wrestling match. But then he saved my life, and the balance was restored. Now he believes it is gone again.

"All things happen for a reason," Sensei says. "One day Yoshi will find a reason for this. The captain has gone, and we must travel on alone."

Our teacher usually lectures with silly stories, strange tales, and sometimes a sharp tap from his staff. But never with such serious words. We've lost more than the captain. For the moment Yoshi is not here either. He has returned to that dark place where Sensei first found him.

"What we cannot change we must accept," Sensei says.

Not me. I don't accept it at all. I want to kick against the boat. I wish I had two legs so I could do it twice as hard. Tears stream down my face. You cannot fight against feelings. Not even a samurai blade can do that.

Above us, the mast creaks. *Crick-crack.* Something

snaps in the wind. Sailcloth billows, eerie and murderous in the moonlight. *Whoosh.* The first sail swings forward. Instinctively, we drop to the deck. Back it sweeps, slamming into the roof of the captain's cabin. *Bang!* The bamboo-thatched compartment crushes as easily as an origami box.

"A batten splintered," says Taji. "I heard the tack line fail as well."

The sail is no longer anchored to the block on the deck and, like a swinging sword, cuts its own lethal path above us.

"Stay low," Sensei commands.

We obey without question. It's good advice if you don't want to lose your head.

Sensei surveys the damaged batten. My head stays down, but my eyes train upward. One of the horizontal bamboo poles running across the sail has broken in two.

"Should we drop the sails?" I ask.

Sensei shakes his head. "First, we must secure the line," he decides. "Mikko, do you still have the rope?"

"I can get it," he answers, voice shaking. "I left it near the ladder."

Face almost flat against the deck, Mikko crawls away

from us. Beneath the hull, the ocean rises and swells. The Striped Gecko scrabbles against the pitch of the deck, but it's too slippery. Mikko slides with a hard thump into the side of the boat.

"Are you all right?" I call.

"I've got the rope," he says. "I landed on top of it."

I'm not even tempted to make a joke. Not tonight. Tonight I am reminded how brave he can be.

"We will also need some strong twine to lash the batten pieces together," says Sensei.

The sail careens toward us again, and the hull rolls to the left. Even our boat has lost its balance. If we don't repair the damage quickly, we'll all be tipped into the sea. Lightning flares to reveal the ocean's great mouth, open in anticipation.

Gripping my arm, Kyoko digs her fingernails deep into my skin. I don't complain, not even when the salt water stings the wound. I know how she feels, because I'm scared, too.

But fear also makes us desperate. And desperation gives us courage.

"I'll find the twine." Taji scrambles across the deck toward the stern.

That leaves four of us to catch the sail and tie it back. Maybe three. Yoshi's head is tucked in his arms, and he hasn't even looked up to see what is happening.

Whoosh. Whoosh. The sail swoops like owl wings, only a thousand times noisier. I feel like a mouse waiting for the owl to strike, only a thousand times more frightened.

Sensei says a samurai must know more than the sword and the bow. Luckily, our teacher is also a skilled shipmaster. In the days before Sensei came to the mountains to build the Cockroach Ryu, he spent many years sailing with Captain Oong's father.

"Throw the end loop around the boom," Sensei says, passing the rope to Kyoko.

Kyoko can throw a *shuriken* star to wedge in the center of a thin bamboo pole, but lassoing this target won't be that easy. The light from the lantern struggles to find its way through the driving rain, and Mikko fights hard to hold the beam steady so Kyoko can see. His arm is strong, but the powerful wind has the storm on its side.

How can three kids and an old man triumph against this gale? Will Yoshi stay huddled into the side of the boat or stir to help us?

"This is not the first time we have fought a Dragon. And we will win again," Sensei promises.

Threading the rope through the block, Sensei knots it tight. He hands the slack to Kyoko.

"You can do this with your eyes closed," I encourage her.

She nods but says nothing. She's not sure. I hold my breath as the rope curls out toward the boom.

And falls with a sodden thud against the deck.

"I missed," Kyoko whispers.

Sensei coils the rope again and hands it to her.

Arm raised, Kyoko hesitates. "What if I miss again?"

"If you miss, it is just practice, and all practice is good," our teacher counsels. "You should take Niya's advice. Close your eyes."

"Like you did when you threw the rope across the chasm in the Tateyama Mountain tunnel," Mikko reminds her.

"Like when you threw the grappling hook across to the Emperor's sleeping quarters," I add.

This time the rope flies like an arrow toward its target. Her confidence is restored; Kyoko doesn't need any more practice.

But we're not safe yet. *Whoosh.* The rope is still too long to hold the sail in place. Using the slack, it continues to sweep back and forth.

Captain Oong would know what to do. The sea was in his blood. But now salt water fills his mouth and the waves flick sand in his ears. I won't let the storm win. It's a matter of honor. The captain's honor.

I'll think of something.

"I know!" I shout triumphantly. "If we loop the slack around the block each time the boom draws closer, we can gradually shorten the rope to secure the sail."

"That'll work," Mikko agrees.

"It's a good idea, Niya," Sensei says.

Yoshi says nothing. He's still crumpled against the side of the deck. He's lost inside himself, but we'll have to wait to bring him back.

Working quickly, we loop and pull each new knot tight.

By the time Taji returns, we have the sail tied almost as securely as before. Taji hands Kyoko the twine. I look up to where she will climb, and my stomach lurches. Not even the White Crane would build its nest that far up.

Kyoko isn't worried. With the twine in her teeth, she scales the rigging like a snow monkey. The mast bends and sways in the wind, but it can't shake her free.

"I wish she'd hurry up and come down," I mutter. "Maybe we should just reef the sails."

"We must keep the boat moving toward our destination," Sensei says. "We have no time to stand still. But don't worry: the wind will weaken soon."

"How do you know?" asks Taji.

Our teacher laughs — a deep belly rumble that rolls with the thunder. "No dragon can bluster and blow forever. And one that tries to swallow Yoshi will certainly get a stomachache and need to rest."

Thump. Kyoko drops from the mast and lands on the deck beside me. For the moment we are all safe. Free to mourn the captain and help Yoshi heal. I turn to tell Yoshi that we can carry him to bed now. But Yoshi is already snoring, exhausted beyond even the blackest memory.

The mast bends and sways in the wind,
but it can't shake her free.

By daybreak the sea slaps at the hull, but sunrise has chased the storm away.

Our boat is a small Chinese junk. Two large cloth sails catch the wind to carry us forward. Yesterday there were three raised compartments in the middle of the boat: one for the captain, one for Sensei, and the other for us. This morning the captain's cabin sprawls, crushed and flattened, but that doesn't matter. It's empty now. I pull my jacket up around my ears and I wish I was inside our warm cabin. The storm's anger is gone, but the wind still bullies our sails with powerful gusts. The Dragon might be sleeping, but it tosses and turns.

I keep expecting to hear the captain's voice roar across the deck, distributing the day's work, telling a joke, or challenging us to speak to him in Chinese. Sensei teaches us many languages with lots of lessons about grammar and pronunciation. But Captain Oong taught us words that weren't in any of Sensei's classes.

"I wish the captain was here," Kyoko whispers.

We all do.

"Tomorrow we will hold a ceremony for Captain Oong," announces Sensei. "It is time to let him go. There are new challenges ahead of us, and our captain would not want us looking back."

I glance at Yoshi; his lips are pressed together. There's a new hardness etched across his face. But I'm not fooled. It's a fragile mask.

Sensei notices, too, but he doesn't pause. "Now that we have almost reached our destination, we will speak only in Chinese," he says.

Mikko groans, but the captain would have approved.

Leaning over the bow, I look out into the endless ocean. Our travels began with trepidation and excitement, but those feelings are gone now. I wish we had stayed at home.

"Why did we come here?" I ask.

"I am broadening your horizons," Sensei answers.

At home the horizon rises and falls with mountain peaks. Here, it stretches forever, from one side of my world to the other. It's never been so broad. But why did the captain have to die? And why did Yoshi have to suffer all over again? Inside my head, I scream at Sensei, *Why? Why?*

"Suffering makes us strong," murmurs Sensei.

I turn to snap in anger. I don't want to be strong. But when I look into the wizard's bright-blue eyes, I see his great strength and all the suffering that made him wise.

Instead of yelling, I bury my head against my master's chest.

Sensei lifts my chin to look into my eyes. "It is time for me to tell a story."

Sitting down, he claps his hands. Quickly, we form a half circle around him, tucking our feet beneath us. There's only one thing better than honey rice pudding, and that's a good story. Of course, it's better to have both, but Yoshi still looks a little green and I wouldn't wave a bowl under his nose yet.

"For me, this journey began before you were born. I voyaged across the ocean with Captain Oong's father and traveled to the Imperial Jade Palace to study."

It's the first story Sensei has ever told us in Chinese. He stops to see if we understand.

"Go on," I want to say, but Sensei teaches us to be patient.

"I visited the White Tiger Temple, where the Shaolin monks are skilled fighters and healers." He pauses to scratch his nose.

Sometimes it is really hard to be patient.

"I stayed for five years. When I left, I promised the abbot I would return if the temple needed my help. And that I would bring with me the best students I could find."

We smile, thinking we are the best. But Sensei hasn't finished his story.

"When we were at Toyozawa Castle, I received a message that the temple has lost its imperial protection and is under threat from jealous military factions. The abbot needs our help as soon as possible. But getting there will be far more perilous than traveling across the ocean. There is a man standing in my way."

It's hard to imagine one man causing Sensei a problem.

"Who?" Kyoko asks.

"His name is Qing-Shen. Once he was my student, just like you. He recently sent me a message." Sensei takes a piece of silk from his pocket and unfolds it to reveal a calligraphy character. It's harder to read Chinese than to speak it, but I recognize the word right away. *Eagle.*

"What does that mean?" asks Taji, puzzled.

"He wants to soar like the Eagle, to rise above all other men. But the Eagle is not his spirit guide, and you cannot force what you must wait to find."

Yoshi nods. He waited much longer than the rest of us to find his spirit guide, but eventually the Tiger tracked him down.

Our master looks sad and closes his eyes, remembering something. "Qing-Shen thinks I deceived him long ago, and now he wants revenge. I expect he would like to see me dead."

That's nothing new, I think.

"When the Emperor of Japan wanted to chop off your head, he soon found out it couldn't be done," Yoshi says.

Mikko nods. "If the Emperor failed, then Qing-Shen doesn't stand a chance."

"Our emperor has a good heart," Sensei says. "But there is nothing good in the dark heart of China's Warrior."

"Is he dangerous?" Kyoko asks.

"He was the most skilled soldier in the Middle Kingdom." Our teacher sighs. "And then I taught him everything I knew."

Could there be anyone more dangerous than that?

CHAPTER THREE

名誉

THE FUNERAL

The shadow of Qing-Shen hangs low over our heads, but Sensei doesn't want to talk about him anymore. I tried to ask about him this morning, but our teacher shook his head. "When we get to China," he promised.

For the third day, the ocean tumbles and turns, taking our stomachs with it. His face pale and gaunt, Yoshi feels it most, groaning with each roll of the ocean.

"Would you like me to get you a cup of water?" Kyoko asks.

"Uuuurgh," he moans, rising to stagger to the side of the boat.

Yoshi is big and solid, like a giant oak, but now he bends like a thin sapling. Crumpled over the port side, his face pale and his knuckles white, he empties his stomach into the sea.

"What a waste of good breakfast." Mikko chuckles and clutches his stomach, too.

I try not to laugh, but I can't help it and even Yoshi manages a weak smile, but Kyoko doesn't think it's funny at all. She glares at Mikko and me, stretching up to put her arms around Yoshi's broad shoulders. "I'll get Sensei. He will help you."

Sensei comes immediately.

30

"It's better to have an empty stomach than an empty head," our teacher reproves, tapping Mikko on the skull with his traveling staff.

"Show me your hand," Sensei tells Yoshi.

I raise my eyebrows, and Mikko shrugs. Taji listens quietly while Kyoko bends closer, concerned. As the ship lurches in the wind, Yoshi retches again, too sick to care what Sensei is saying. Maybe seasickness is a good thing. At least Yoshi isn't thinking about the captain.

"Help him lie down," instructs Sensei.

It takes all four of us to pry Yoshi's barnacle grip from the side of the boat and lay him gently on the deck.

Our teacher turns his patient's palm to the overcast sky, and his thumbs gently knead the skin on Yoshi's wrist. Yoshi grimaces. How can it be a cure when he now hurts in two places instead of one?

"How do you feel?" asks Sensei.

Yoshi groans. "Like a dead fish."

I bite my lip; I won't laugh again with Kyoko watching.

"When I press here on Yoshi's wrist, his *ki* energy moves forward," Sensei explains. "If his *ki* is strong enough, it will win the battle raging in his stomach."

Yoshi's *ki is* powerful. Just like mine. Taji's, Mikko's, Kyoko's, and Nezume's, too. Combined, our *ki* can change even the Emperor's mind. That's how we rescued Sensei when he was imprisoned at Toyozawa Castle.

Sensei passes Yoshi's hand over to Kyoko. Carefully, she presses her fingers against his wrist.

I'm sure that would make *me* feel better. And it works for Yoshi, too. He sits up. His face is still pale, but a thin half-moon smile beams across it.

"I'm hungry," he growls, rubbing his empty stomach.

It's a miracle cure. On a different morning, I'd launch myself at Yoshi and wrestle him to the ground. But now I'm just glad to see him happy again.

"First," Sensei continues, "we must work. We have repairs to make, provisions to count, and lessons to catch up."

"Work, work, work," Mikko grumps. "Even in the middle of the ocean, we're always working and practicing."

"There is much to learn," Sensei says. "All my students are destined to go far."

He says that all the time, but none of us ever imagined he meant so far across the sea.

"A rolling ocean is the perfect training ground to practice balancing skills. After all, it is not good to fall on your own blade."

It's true. But it's not good getting to our feet, either. We struggle to rise as the boat pitches forward.

Yoshi groans, and Mikko slips, thumping down beside him. I slide into Taji, and Kyoko slams into me, knocking us all to the deck. Only Sensei is still standing. It takes more than the ground shifting to move Sensei.

"Uuuurgh." It's Mikko's turn to heave over the side of the boat. I bet he doesn't think it's funny now.

Bong. Bong.

Sensei uses a heavy soup ladle to sound the funeral gong that Mikko made by flattening a cooking pot. He strikes it twice so the captain will have an easy path into the next life. In China, where Captain Oong was born, two is a lucky number. He told us it meant that life would be easy and that good things always came in pairs.

But two hasn't been lucky for us. First, the captain

drowned, and then part of Yoshi died trying to save him. That's a pair of disasters.

I've been to only one funeral before this. Still, I know it's important to have a body to pay last respects to, before fire purifies the soul and the flesh returns to the earth. But Captain Oong's body sank to the bottom of the sea.

Old men, like my grandfather, say a man walks the earth forever if he's not buried properly. A heavy weight of ocean presses hard against the captain's chest. Surely no ghost could rise from under that.

It's Yoshi's spirit that worries me more. His face is pale and his eyes are miles away.

I tug on his jacket to attract his attention. "Are you feeling all right?"

"As long as I don't eat anything." Patting his stomach, Yoshi manages a weak grin.

It's not what I meant, and he knows it. This funeral gives us a chance to say good-bye, and now hopefully Yoshi can let go of his grief.

"It's my fault we're here," he mutters.

Bong. Bong, the gong interrupts.

"We stand before Heaven to honor the journey of

our friend from this world to the next," Sensei intones, raising his hands into the wind. His kimono sleeves billow like sails around thin, mastlike arms.

A shadow passes over the deck. Above us, a large white bird with black-tipped wings settles at the top of the rigging. We've seen many albatrosses on our voyage, but none have landed on the boat before. Eye cocked in Sensei's direction, it listens closely.

"Maybe it's the captain," murmurs Kyoko. "Some sailors believe the albatross is the soul of a lost seafarer."

"Don't be silly," Mikko says. "It's just a bird."

"Captain Oong's body drifts beneath the boat. Maybe his soul is lost with it," suggests Taji.

"What do you think, Niya?" Worried, Yoshi looks to me for support.

"It doesn't matter," I insist. "This funeral will ensure the captain finds peace." And Yoshi, too.

Sensei says funerals are not really for the dead. They are for those left behind. "The dead are long gone by the time a funeral is held," he told us. "Who would wait when the doors of Heaven are open? Only the living would be foolish enough to still hang around on earth."

The captain wouldn't be hanging around at all. He

liked to get things done. Even better, he liked to bark orders at us. That got things done with a lot less effort from him.

Captain Oong was a big, friendly man. His beard was as spiky as a sea urchin and matted with salt. His left eye was an empty socket, the eyeball caught on a fishhook and abandoned somewhere on the bottom of the ocean. The captain could lift a barrel of drinking water with his right arm and Kyoko with the other.

We liked him a lot.

Bong. Bong.

Sensei strikes the gong again. It calls to the ocean, and it calls to the sky. It calls the captain home.

"Captain Oong was a good son," Sensei proclaims. "He made his ancestors proud."

We take turns to say something to commend the captain to his next life.

"Captain Oong taught me where to find all the stars," Taji whispers.

He was very patient.

"Captain Oong had a sense of humor," Mikko says. "He laughed at all my jokes."

He was very kind.

"Captain Oong was a great adventurer," I add.

He was very brave.

"He was not old. His body was strong and healthy," says Yoshi.

The captain was too young to die.

Kyoko sniffs, unable to speak. Sometimes saying nothing means most of all.

I place my hand on her arm. "You were like a daughter to him. You had the captain wrapped around all your fingers."

Kyoko sniffs again, wiping her nose along her kimono sleeve. There's nothing ladylike about a samurai girl. And samurai kids are not always brave. Tears glisten in the corner of Yoshi's eyes. Mikko bites his lip hard, and Taji blinks wet lashes. I struggle not to cry.

Sensei opens a basket of origami figures. We made them yesterday to take our minds off the roll of the waves. Every time the boat pitched, monkeys clambered, geckos scuttled, tigers pounced, bats swooped, and the white crane flew. All across the cabin, from one side to the other.

Now Sensei holds the basket out for us to toss the paper creatures into the ocean. Then our spirit guides will help the captain find his way.

Bong. Bong.

Sensei strikes the gong for the final time and bows three times toward the east. The ceremony is over.

"Om-om-om." His voice soars upward, and the White Crane rises to meet it as we chant in unison. *"Om-om."* It's a sound loud enough to overpower the wind.

And, as if by magic, it does.

An eerie quiet rolls over the ocean. The wind drops onto all fours and crawls away. Dark clouds part as the sun wields its own sword stroke through the heavens. The froth on the waves dissolves into spit bubbles.

"What happened?" I ask nervously.

Laughing, Sensei snorts the salt from his nose. "The Dragon finally sleeps untroubled. It must have tired of making my students miserable. Or perhaps after our ceremony, the captain no longer lies on the seabed poking dragon ribs."

The change unsettles the albatross, too. It spreads its wings and soars off toward the horizon.

"I'm sure it was the captain," Kyoko insists.

It's unusual for her to believe something like that. The women in the village below our *ryu* gossip that Sensei is a *tengu,* a mountain goblin priest who can change into a black demon-crow whenever he wants. There are many things about Sensei I can't explain and sometimes I'm tempted to believe the stories. But my friends think that's silly and laugh at me.

Sensei says nothing, his smile almost as wide as the ocean.

"The seafarer's soul has found its way home," I whisper to Yoshi.

But now we have a new problem.

"How will we travel with no wind in our sails?" Taji asks. "We can't flap our wings and fly like an albatross."

A Chinese junk needs only a breath of air, but there is not even that.

"It seems for a while we are going nowhere," Sensei agrees.

"What will we do?" Kyoko licks a finger and holds it high, hoping for wind. "The White Tiger Temple is waiting for us."

"We cannot go with the flow when nothing is moving," I say.

Sensei taps the deck with his staff. "It does not matter whether we are on land or sea, in the classroom or in a boat. Whenever we have spare time, we should practice. Then we will be of even greater use to the temple when we arrive."

And more prepared to meet Qing-Shen.

"Hurrah." Mikko unsheathes his sword and waves it wildly.

"Wooden *bokken*s only," Sensei reminds him. "We do not need to lose any more arms and legs."

"We'll be very careful," Mikko says, eager to slash his blade in the sunlight.

Our teacher shakes his head. "How many times has Taji broken Niya's nose?"

I wince. Four times and as recently as a month ago.

"Too many," I say. Beside me, Taji chuckles unsympathetically.

"If we use real swords, Niya might lose his nose," Sensei says.

There's no arguing with that.

But it's hard to find the place to start our lesson. This is the first time we've practiced swordsmanship since we left Nezume at Toyozawa Castle. We're one kid short.

Mikko and Nezume, our best swordsmen, usually train together, but Nezume lives in the Emperor's castle now, teaching the prince swordsmanship. And Mikko hasn't got a partner.

"I wish Nezume was here," Kyoko says softly.

"For now, Nezume follows his own path. But all paths lead to the center, and one day we will meet up again," promises Sensei. "What would Nezume say if he *was* here?"

"More practice!" we shout together.

Sensei nods, pleased. "I will be Mikko's partner."

Our teacher is stick-figure thin and very old. You can see where his bones press against the skin. But he wields his sword like lightning, and its blade can pass through younger bones stacked three men deep.

"I'll go with Yoshi," I volunteer. I don't want to risk sparring with Taji today, and Yoshi might need me.

Yoshi won't swing his blade in a fight, but he's happy to block practice sword strokes. He doesn't take the offensive, but it's still excellent training trying to discover a chink in his defense.

But today Yoshi's heart is not in swordplay, and I easily land three points in quick succession.

"Let's have a rest," I say, sitting with my back against the side of the boat.

Yoshi flops next to me.

"What's wrong, Yosh?"

Coughing to clear his throat, Yoshi finds his voice, raspy and shaking. "Why can't things ever go right for me?" he whispers.

I know Sensei will have heard, and I look across to him for advice.

You know what to say. Sensei's words echo in my brain.

He needs your help, I plead. *You are his teacher. You are like a father to him.*

Sensei disagrees. *He does not need a father now. He needs a brother. Search your heart, and you will find what to say.*

Yoshi looks at me hopefully, waiting for an answer.

Closing my eyes, I feel the White Crane reach its wings toward me. "Each warrior must follow the path in front of him," I say. "Things cannot always go right." I lean closer to whisper in his ear. "Sometimes they must go left. It's hard to go right when you only have a left foot."

Yoshi almost smiles at my joke.

I hook my arm around his shoulder. It's not an easy

reach; Yoshi is much bigger than me. But at this moment, inside, he's really small.

"You and I are blood brothers. We are always on the same path," I tell him. "That night on the mountain, you were there for me when I fell, and I will always be here for you."

He nods.

I can read my friend's face like a rice-paper scroll. Yoshi still feels small, but he no longer feels alone.

"The weather is changing." Sensei holds his beard into the breeze. "The wind is gently gusting, and the sea is no longer fighting against us. Finally, the Dragon has given our journey its blessing."

Yoshi scowls. "It is hardly a fair payment for our captain."

The sea has changed Yoshi. It has left him hard and brittle around the edges. Even the captain's funeral was not enough to soften the pain.

Inside me, the White Crane huddles close, seeking comfort. *Please don't let Yoshi break.*

Sometimes a mended pot is even stronger than before, Sensei advises. *But you cannot restore a pot all in one day. After the pieces are joined together, you must wait for the lacquer to set.*

Perhaps this is the best way to honor
Captain Oong.

It's hard to be patient when a friend is hurting.

Mikko heads for the rudder mounted in the stern, and Taji follows. It takes two kids to move it even a little. Yoshi slackens the rope collar that fastens the wooden forward-edge spar. Slowly, the sails move toward the line of the ship as we head into the wind.

Perhaps this is the best way to honor Captain Oong. To prove how well we learned the skills he taught us.

"Look!" Kyoko yells.

I follow her pointing finger. To where the ocean ends.

"We're on our way to the White Tiger Temple." Mikko whoops, eager to begin our mission.

"What about Qing-Shen?" Kyoko reminds him.

"We'll deal with him when we have to," Mikko blusters. "He's not waiting for us on the shore."

Taji nods, but I'm not so certain. Just because there are no cliffs doesn't mean there is no Eagle. Beside me, Yoshi is concentrating hard.

"What do you think, Yosh?" I ask.

The Tiger growls softly. "He'll come. I can feel him."

I look over to Sensei, but for once he is not listening. Staring toward China, he is already miles away.

CHAPTER FOUR

忠
誠

THE DRAGON'S
BACK

"The Land of the Dragon," Sensei proclaims, thumping his staff into the marshy tangle of roots and reeds.

It seems we are never to be free of the Dragon. I roll up my trousers and dig my foot into the sand. I imagine I am burying my toenail into the soft skin between dragon scales.

For weeks I've dreamed of being on dry earth again. But this land is soggy and wet, sticky and salty. With lakes and puddles as far as I can see. There is nothing familiar, and already I am homesick for our mountains.

We don't belong here.

Kyoko can sense it, too. "What if they don't like us?"

"Who?" Mikko asks.

"The Chinese people. What if they don't like strangers? They might think we look funny."

Taji smiles. "We've always looked strange. And the way Mikko speaks Chinese is definitely funny. No one will be able to understand him, but I'm sure they'll still like him anyway."

We laugh, but underneath we are all nervous of what this land will bring. Of Qing-Shen and the task that awaits us at the temple.

"People are always afraid of anything different. They

are afraid of change," says Sensei. "It is the same every-where."

"Captain Oong would be glad to be here," mutters Yoshi.

"You're right, and we are lucky to be here, too," I say. "At least we know we are welcome at the temple."

"I won't fight at the temple," Yoshi whispers.

"You won't have to. The temple is not looking for defenders. It already has many of those," says Sensei. "It is looking to hide away its treasures so when the raiders come, there is nothing left to be stolen."

"Is it far to the temple?" Taji asks.

"About ten days," replies our master.

Taji doesn't ask the other question. The one we all want to know. Sensei hasn't mentioned his old student, not since Captain Oong's funeral. He will tell us more when he is ready, but I'm ready now.

"Where is China's Warrior?" I ask. "Will he find us soon?"

"He is waiting for the right moment to challenge me."

"But you can beat him, can't you, Sensei?" Kyoko asks nervously, threading her hair through her fingers.

Our teacher grins. "With my eyes shut and one hand tied behind my back."

Once Sensei told us there was a long line of men waiting for his head. But they all failed. Even the Emperor and the Dragon Master. Why should this man be any different?

"I was worried he might kill you," admits Kyoko.

"Anything is possible, but I am in more danger of catching a chill standing here in the sludge," Sensei says. "Chop, chop, Little Cockroaches. We can only take with us what we can easily carry."

For the moment, our master isn't going to tell us any more about Qing-Shen. But even though he doesn't seem worried, I can't shake the feeling of unease that tugs at the White Crane's feathers. What if being able to win the fight is not enough?

"What will we do about the boat?" Yoshi asks.

"It will be safe anchored here," Sensei says. "We do not need her now. We have a short walk ahead but a long ride. Decide carefully what to bring. I do not want the horses overburdened."

What horses? We are surrounded by wetlands. Birds,

crabs, and I'm sure eels are hunting somewhere not too far from my toes, but there's not a horse in sight.

"Where will we get the horses from?" Mikko looks around.

"From the village, of course." Sensei smiles, daring us to ask the next question.

Kyoko rises to the challenge.

"Where is the village? There is nothing here but sand and mud." She flicks a footful in my direction.

"We will find a large settlement a few hours away. An easy walk for students who need to exercise and stretch their legs after lazy weeks at sea."

There's still one catch. Even if we find a village and they do have six horses, how will we pay? A samurai doesn't work for gold and silver; he wields his sword for honor. But honor won't buy many horses.

"How can we afford horses?" I ask. "We have no money."

Sensei's eyes gleam. "Perhaps we will find we have a boat to trade."

This morning is filled with question marks. Without a boat, how will we get home? But I trust Sensei, and

I'm not sorry to leave the boat and its memories behind. I bet Yoshi feels the same.

"Hurry, hurry." Sensei claps his hands. "Time to pack."

"We'll need food," says Mikko. "I'll get that."

"Rice rolls, dried fish, and noodles. Bring it all," calls Yoshi.

Already, we don't trust this land. Not even to feed us.

"You'll get fat," I tease my friend. "I feel sorry for your horse."

Yoshi feints a playful punch, but I'm careful to dodge anyway. Even a light clip on the ears from him stings more than a swat from Sensei's staff. But I'm so pleased to see Yoshi laughing that I wouldn't mind at all.

"We'll need a change of clothes and spare sandals," Kyoko says.

Taji has our packs out.

"And the gong," adds Sensei.

"Do we really need that?" questions Yoshi.

"Yes," Sensei insists. "And raincoats."

"And rope, a cooking pot, blankets . . ." I'm good at making lists. Sensei says when the body is incomplete, the mind grows to compensate. I don't run very fast, but

I think quicker than my two-legged friends. Even faster than Sensei, although I'd never say it aloud.

I heard anyway, my wizard teacher whispers inside my head.

Sometimes I forget he can do that.

Sorry, Sensei, I whisper back, hanging my head.

He laughs. "One day you will do many things more swiftly than me, and I will be able to rest more often."

Hardly likely. Sensei's wisdom is wider then the Sea of Japan and deeper than any ocean. He definitely doesn't need more time to sleep. He's always snoring somewhere. Even now he searches out a dry tussock to sit cross-legged, eyes closed, while we organize the supplies.

We work briskly, gathering and sorting everything into piles.

"Look!" Kyoko yells, her voice rising with excitement.

Standing on one leg in the salty water is a tall, stately bird with a bright-red crest on its head. It fishes, oblivious to Kyoko's shouting.

"Every winter, the red crane comes here to the eastern marshlands to breed." Sensei is teaching another lesson.

And part of it is just for me. The crane belongs here in

the Land of the Dragon. As I watch, the red crane turns to look in my direction, and deep inside, the White Crane dips its head in acknowledgment.

With a flurry of feathers and wings opened wide, the bird lifts itself into the air. Screeching once, it heads west.

"That's where we are going," says Sensei. "Are we ready?"

Kyoko has tied all our supplies into clever bundles, her Snow Monkey fingers working magic with knots and string. Yoshi's bundle is twice the size of ours, but he throws it over his shoulder as easily as if it were empty.

"How do you know which way to go?" Yoshi asks.

"I follow my nose," says Sensei.

Mikko laughs. "But it's always in front of you."

"Exactly," Sensei says, striding off after his nose.

Sensei's nose soon finds its way to a well-worn path. The ground hardens beneath my sandal and the mud dries between my toes. We haven't gone far before Taji stops.

"Someone is coming," he announces.

"Not someone, but something," Sensei corrects.

A ripple furrows across the lake on our right. Two

ears, soft eyes, an elongated face, and two sharp tusks draw closer.

"What is it?" Kyoko asks, admiring.

"It is a water deer," Sensei replies. "You will see many new things on this journey. It is a good way to learn."

Mikko grins. He likes that. The Striped Gecko doesn't like to sit in the classroom, but it's happy to run along the road.

"Why is the deer coming to you, Sensei?" Kyoko puzzles.

It's a ridiculous thing to say, but it's true. The deer is swimming purposefully to the lake edge nearest our teacher. It shakes the drips from its coat and steps out of the marsh reeds with its head lowered, waiting for Sensei to approach.

Our teacher looks in its mouth, behind its tusks, and up its nose, then carefully bends back each ear.

"What's he doing?" Yoshi whispers.

"Asking where it hurts," explains Kyoko.

Just because she helps Sensei mix potions for the villagers doesn't mean she can trick us into believing he talks to animals.

Mikko snickers. I can't help joining in his laughter.

"No way," I say.

"Sometimes you are the smartest boy I know." She smiles.

I grin.

"And sometimes"— she whacks me across the ears — "you are such a birdbrain."

When I look back, Sensei is rubbing a salve under the deer's chin.

"You were right," I mutter, red-faced, as the deer returns to the water.

"What was all the laughing about?" Sensei asks, looking at me. As if he doesn't know.

"Kyoko was teaching Niya a lesson," Taji says. Mikko laughs and Yoshi pokes me in the ribs. Kyoko giggles. You can't fight feelings, and you can't fight laughter, either.

Sensei walks in front. The monotonous slap of sandals counts the minutes. The minutes drag into half hours and the half hours stretch out forever.

"It's so flat, I can see for miles," says Yoshi, marveling.

"Not much use when there's nothing to see," I grump.

I'm tired of walking through this boring countryside, and my foot aches.

"There is always something to see. Even if you do not look, it will find you in the end," our master says.

"*Ouch!*" I shout, and clutch at the pebble wedged between my toes.

"Let's see." Kyoko reaches out to help me. "Something found you when you weren't looking."

I fling the pebble as far along the path as I can. A puff of dust marks its landing spot.

"A ripple begins with a pebble," Sensei murmurs.

And so does a bruise on my foot. I'm glad we're no longer sloshing through puddles, but we haven't escaped the water yet. It's everywhere around us. Even now an irrigation ditch flows beside the path.

"There's the village!" shouts Taji.

Yoshi scratches his head. "I can't see anything."

I search and eventually spot a smudge in the distance. "Got it!" I yell.

"How did *you* know where it was?" Kyoko asks Taji.

"A village has many smells, and they are making an excellent lunch at the one we are heading toward."

Good. I'm tired of dried fish, pickled vegetables, and rice. Chasing the possibility of a tasty meal, we cover the distance quickly.

At the edge of the village, a noisy crowd is waiting — men, women, and little children who poke their heads out from behind their mothers' baggy pants. Dogs bark, geese honk, ducks with shiny green feathers quack, and one well-fed pig pushes its way through to greet us.

"Perhaps they have heard that a group of great samurai warriors is coming to save the White Tiger Temple." Mikko grins at the pig. "I see the village dignitaries are here."

"We must watch our words and mind our manners," Sensei reproves. "This is not Japan. And you must remember that it is rude not to speak in Chinese."

I stifle a giggle. It's probably a good thing no one understood what Mikko said.

"Sorry, Sensei." Mikko hangs his head. "I didn't mean to offend."

"I understand." Sensei lifts Mikko's chin and smiles. "But here, it is our ways that are strange and we must always be aware of that. Heads are easily lost to careless words."

Stepping forward, a large man holds out his hands in greeting. He's not quite as tall as Sensei but twice as wide. He wears a thickly embroidered jacket, and a large gold pendant hangs around his neck. But his hands are weathered and his back slightly stooped. This man holds an important position yet has worked hard all his life.

"Welcome, Ki-Yaga," the village chief says.

Our teacher is a legendary samurai swordsman. Even the Land of the Dragon knows his name.

Sensei bows low. He respects this man a great deal. "Greetings, old friend."

"What brings you to my humble village?" the man asks.

"I bear sad tidings, Zhou. We were three days from the coast when a great storm attacked. Your brother Oong fell overboard and perished." Sensei bows again. "One of my students attempted to rescue him, but the sea would not give back her prize. We nearly lost two lives that night."

Sensei's words fall like a heavy weight, and the chief's face contorts with pain. Grief lines spread like ripples in a pond as the stone sinks in. The villagers drift back to work, leaving their chief to mourn.

My grandfather once told me the story of how a gigantic wave rose from the seabed to swallow the land and its people for many days. Then it spat them out again. Surrounded by mountains and hills, I found Grandfather's tale hard to believe. But it's easier to imagine here on the endless flat plain. Especially now. The silence rears like a great tsunami, threatening to wash us away.

Will the chief blame us for his brother's death? What punishment will fall on our heads? Maybe we will no longer have heads at all.

Finally, Zhou speaks. "My brother would not have been happy under the ground. Now that his life has ended, it is right that his body rests under the sea." Zhou struggles to stop his voice from shaking. "What happened to his boat?"

"I have moored it in the marshes near where the red cranes gather."

Zhou nods approvingly. "Then I gift my brother's vessel to the student who tried to save his life."

Yoshi owns a boat!

But not for long.

"My student has no need of a boat," Sensei says. "He would gladly accept six horses with strong legs."

Zhou smiles. Even grieving, the chief has a village to feed, and a boat is far more valuable than six horses. It is a good deal firmly weighted in his favor.

"Then I will give you some traveling advice," he says. "There is much change in China. Be twice as wary as you grow closer to the Yellow River. It is hard to tell friend from enemy unless you know their name."

I'm not worried; Sensei knows many names, and many know his. Just as this village chief did.

"Thank you." Sensei bows again. "Your advice is worth its weight in gold."

"Then perhaps I should be paid for it." Zhou grins, rubbing his hands together.

Sensei grins, too. "And perhaps I already did. Only you can determine how much my compliment is worth."

Zhou laughs until his belly shakes and his jacket strains against its buttons. "Even though your news is not good, you and your students are always welcome here. Come. We will celebrate our friendship with a meal."

"I'm starving," Yoshi whispers, rubbing his stomach as he leads us after Sensei and Zhou.

The chief turns, surprised. "Your Chinese is excellent," he commends Yoshi. "You speak as if you were born here."

Yoshi bows respectfully. "Your brother spent many hours teaching us. We are in his debt."

"And I am grateful that my brother spent his last journey in such good company." The chief turns back to Sensei, who smiles. Pleased and proud.

I smile, too. Yoshi is coming back to us. He is almost here.

The village is a large group of thatched houses clustered around a clearing. In the center is a well, where girls draw water and empty it into round wooden bowls. Seeing us, they disappear into nearby doorways, laughing behind their hands.

"This way." Zhou guides us toward the house closest to the well. "Until you are ready to leave, please consider this your home."

In the morning, the sun rises, and the day is hot and humid. I'm glad we'll be riding today. After a breakfast of dumplings and soup, Zhou calls us to the village center. Beside the well, a girl waits with seven horses. Perhaps Sensei will be allowed to choose the best six.

"I am a man of honor," Zhou says. "I cannot accept my brother's boat in exchange for only six horses. I will also supply this guide to see you safely across the Northern Plain."

What? We don't need a guide. Especially if it's a girl. Kyoko doesn't count because she's one of us. We don't have to look after her. But this new girl will just slow us down.

Sensei steps forward to tell the chief we don't need her help.

"Thank you," he says. "We are very pleased to have your youngest daughter accompany us. We need to make haste, and her directions will help us travel faster. It is many years since I visited the temple, and I have found that paths always change."

Zhou slaps him on the back. "It solves a problem for me, too. My daughter Mei-Ying prefers to spend her time riding and practicing Shaolin fighting. No man

will marry a woman who can toss him to the ground."
Zhou shakes his head with a father's loving exasperation.
"But she could find the way to the White Tiger Temple
with her eyes closed, and that will be useful." Then his
voice drops to a whisper. "Look after her, Ki-Yaga."

Sensei nods. "She is in many good hands." His gaze
sweeps across us all, but I pretend not to notice. I'm not
going to look after a girl.

I turn to my friends, expecting them to feel the same.
But Kyoko is beaming as if she's found a new friend.
Yoshi looks bemused. Taji too. And Mikko is always
happy to grin at a girl.

Mei-Ying has long black hair, broad shoulders, and
smiling dark eyes that shine like polished river stone.
It's impossible to glare at her. Hypnotized, I smile back.

"I have something else for you all." Zhou hands Sensei
a large package. "It is a tent. Oong gave it to me on his
last visit. I hear it can be tricky to build, but I am sure
you will find it useful."

"Thank you. It is a most welcome gift." Sensei looks
skyward, where the clouds are already gathering. "I have
not forgotten the summer storms."

64

Mei-Ying passes me the reins to a horse. I'm a good rider. Like my friends, I learned the hard way, on Uma, Sensei's cantankerous old warhorse. This horse is smaller than Uma, but solid and muscular, perfect for the long journey ahead. Her coat is a puddle of color, brown like dried fish, cream like tofu, and black like rolled seaweed.

"What's her name?" I ask.

Mei-Ying looks at me, surprised. "She's a workhorse. She doesn't need one."

I'm going to give her one anyway. "Izuru," I whisper into her mane, naming her after the sword of my childhood. I don't have it anymore; I gave it to our ninja friend Riaze. But I never let go of its name. I kept that for something special.

A crowd soon gathers to wave us on our way.

"We wish you safe passage across the Dragon's back," Zhou says, raising his hand in farewell.

Sensei lifts his traveling staff in response. He nudges his bony knees gently into his horse's belly, and it begins to run. Our teacher is in a hurry now.

I wish we could have stayed in the village longer.

"What's her name?" I ask.

Instead, we are riding headlong into an unfamiliar landscape where strangers like us are not wanted and Qing-Shen is a local hero.

So much is unknown. And what I don't know frightens me. The White Crane tucks its head under a wing. It wants to go home. But a samurai must put honor first, and Sensei's promise must be met.

Even if it means that we never return home.

CHAPTER FIVE

義

CANAL SNAKE

The never-ending plain stretches before us. Hour after hour. North, west, south. It runs on and on and on. Sometimes I feel we'll never escape the flatlands and reach the mountains. Maybe this is where Qing-Shen will find us. Here, where there's nowhere to hide.

Sensei's horse stops, and our teacher quickly dismounts.

"What's wrong?" Yoshi asks, reining in beside him.

"It is time to rest the horses. And this will be a good opportunity to catch up on missed lessons."

Mikko groans.

"My students are lazy from too many hours sitting in the saddle." Sensei waves his staff under Mikko's nose. "This morning we will practice sword fighting."

Mikko stops whining then. Sword fighting is his favorite lesson.

We unhook our bags from the horses and pile them in a clump. Sensei settles back against them to sleep. He says he does his best teaching this way and he doesn't need to see what we are doing.

That makes sense to me. There's nothing worse than a teacher looking over your shoulder all the time. When I am doing calligraphy and Sensei stops to look, my page splatters with ink.

Mikko unsheathes his sword and swings it in a perfect arc. He probably doesn't need to practice at all.

Mei-Ying watches with interest. "I could beat any one of you," she says, her eyes bright with challenge. Her accent is hard to understand, but her meaning is easy to work out.

"You could not." Mikko rises to the bait. "You don't even have a sword."

"I don't need one," she says, arms folded, legs splayed.

Yoshi smiles at me and winks. A true samurai doesn't need a sword, either, but someone needs to defend the honor of the Cockroach Ryu against this pushy girl.

"I accept your challenge," I say.

My friends gather around us. Sensei is still asleep, not listening at all.

"Go, Mei!" Kyoko calls.

I glare at her, a traitor in our midst.

"Girls have to stick together." Kyoko pokes her tongue out at me.

"You're lucky I'm not using my sword, or I'd cut that off," I threaten.

Mei stands very still, eyes closed, focusing on something we can't see. She reminds me of Taji, and I remember how he can sometimes beat me even though he can't see where I am. The White Crane isn't going to take this girl for granted.

Motionless, I watch for the first muscle twitch to give away the moment when she will launch herself and the wrestling will begin.

But she's too fast for me. Her leg snakes out and, before I can move, curls itself around my ankle and pulls me to the ground with a thump.

"Poor Niya." Taji shakes his head. "Beaten by a girl."

I don't have to take revenge on Taji. Kyoko reaches over to smack him across the ear. Even the Golden Bat didn't hear that coming.

When Mei offers her hand to help me up, I take it willingly. I'm not ashamed to be beaten by a better opponent, even if it is a girl. Others might have cried "unfair" because Mei didn't make any allowances for my one leg. She pulled it right out from under me. But I like that. She doesn't think one leg makes me weak.

"How did Taji know it was you who fell?" Mei asks, amazed.

Rubbing his ear, Taji is now paying attention again. "It's a sound I hear almost every day. A one-legged *splat* on the ground."

Mei smiles. "A wise man once said, 'The greatest glory is not in never falling but in rising every time we fall.'"

"That sounds like something Sensei would teach," says Kyoko.

"Not likely." Mei laughs. "Confucius died over fifteen hundred years ago. But"—she makes a face—"he left many hundreds of words of wisdom for us to study and learn by heart."

I look at Sensei, snoring away. He's the oldest person I know, but even he's not that old. Still, I bet he and Confucius would have been good friends.

"What's he doing?" Mei points to Yoshi.

Yoshi has left us to sit apart, cross-legged and head down, shoulders sagging.

"When your uncle was washed overboard, Yoshi tried to save him. Yoshi was almost back to safety when a robber wave stole Captain Oong from his grasp. He blames himself for the captain's death."

"He shouldn't," she whispers.

"Sometimes he forgets and everything is all right. But too often, he remembers," I say. "Perhaps you can help." I drop my voice so Kyoko can't hear what I say next. She'd never let me forget it. "Yoshi needs to talk, and girls make the best listeners."

Chattering away to Mikko, Kyoko doesn't hear. But Taji does and winks at me.

"What did you say?" I ask when Mei returns after a few minutes talking with Yoshi.

"I told him to box up his troubles until he is ready to solve them. In China, some people believe you can divide your mind into small compartments and put one problem inside each. Then close the lid. One by one, the boxes are opened later."

"Does it work?" I ask.

She shrugs. "I'm not sure."

Yoshi has rejoined us, laughing at something Mikko said. Perhaps Mei's boxes are working, after all.

Our teacher's eyes snap open. "Lunch," he says, yawning and flexing his feet. But I'm not fooled. He's been listening in all along.

The meal is pasty rice rolls, without even a sliver of fish for flavor. No dipping sauce, either. It fills the belly but offends the taste buds.

"I miss the Tateyama Mountains," Taji says. "It's cool and peaceful there. This plain is too dry and dusty. The dirt gets up my nose."

Here the landscape is tinged yellow-cream with heads of grain, pale tassels of corn and tufts of feather grass. The seeds wedge between my toes and stick into the bottom of my sandal.

"I like the lines," Yoshi says. "The way the canals criss-cross the plain, cutting it into sections and chunks."

Yoshi always likes things in order. Maybe that's why he struggles so hard when his life is out of balance.

"The flatness of the plain is good," says Sensei. "It helps me to observe who is following."

"Is anyone following us now?" Mikko spins around.

"No." Sensei shakes his head. "But Qing-Shen is coming."

Mei looks up in alarm.

"I would like to know more about Qing-Shen," I say. Then maybe I can work out why Mei looks so frightened.

Taking a deep breath, Sensei closes his eyes, finally ready to tell the whole story. "I am not proud of what I must say. I have made two big mistakes in my life, and one of them was Qing-Shen. Soon the time will come for me to pay."

"But I thought all your students were destined for greatness," Yoshi says.

"They are." Sensei nods. "But not all that is great is good. Qing-Shen was sixteen when he came to the Cockroach Ryu. His skill had already made him a hero in China. I thought he was the one I was waiting for."

"To do what?" I question.

"To take my place. But Qing-Shen's skill with the sword belonged to the highest bidder. He chose fortune over honor."

"So why is Qing-Shen angry with you?" Taji asks. "He made his own choices."

"I made him a promise. But when I looked into Qing-Shen's heart, I knew the promise could not be kept."

Sensei is a samurai of the oldest ways. He values his

word almost as much as his sword and his name. Our master takes a promise very seriously. It must have been dark inside Qing-Shen's heart.

"Now that the White Tiger Temple is in danger, Qing-Shen knows I will return to help. He will already be on his way to confront me."

"Will he wait until we reach the temple?" Taji asks.

"I do not know." Sensei shrugs. "He does not care about the temple or its monks. He only cares about himself. He will attack when I am not looking."

I breathe a sigh of relief. Sensei is always looking, back across the plain and forward to the horizon. He is safe for now.

"He'll have to get through us first," says Yoshi. "I'm not afraid of heroes."

"Me, either." I stand beside my friend, ready to defend our teacher. "I'm not afraid of Qing-Shen."

And Yoshi is the only hero for me.

Sensei nods. "Good. I will need your support."

I've seen Sensei take on ten men without even drawing his sword. I can't imagine any man Sensei needs help to manage. In my mind I see a small, dark figure striding quickly toward us. Baring his teeth in a twisted smile, he reaches for the hilt of his sword. The White Crane cringes as the man looks directly at me. Then Yoshi steps in front of him. Even in my imagination, Yoshi comes to my rescue.

"I am glad Qing-Shen is coming," Sensei says. "I need to put things right."

Yoshi nods. He understands and so do I. A cracked pot is much stronger when mended. Even a very old one.

"Time to go," Sensei says. We strap our bags back onto the horses. Izuru nuzzles gently against my hand as I guide her to trot beside Mei. "You are an excellent wrestler," I tell her. "How did you learn to move so fast?"

"After my birth, my mother was very ill. My father spent everything we had on medicine and doctors. Nothing helped. Finally, my father applied to the monks at the White Tiger Temple for a treatment. But by then, he had no money to pay. So he promised to send a son to the abbot when the boy was five."

"Do you have a brother there?" Mikko asks.

"My mother never bore any more children, so to honor his obligation, my father sent me. The Shaolin monks taught me many things—to read and write, to fight to defend myself, and, if necessary, to kill. One day the abbot called me to him and said it was time for me to go home. I didn't want to, but he said I would return when I was needed."

"Is that why your father sent you to guide us?" Yoshi asks from behind.

"No. The abbot asked me not to repeat his words in my village. He said destiny doesn't need help. What must happen, will."

"Yes," Sensei agrees.

He sounds sad.

As the sun moves halfway down toward evening, a long, straight river cuts across our view.

"This is the Great Canal. My people built it," Mei says proudly. "We call it the throat of China because it transports rice from the south and wheat from the north. Food goes down and food comes up."

"Don't say that." Mikko groans.

He must be remembering how his stomach upended itself a few days ago on the boat.

"How are we going to get across?" I ask.

Sensei dismounts and unpacks the gong. "I will find someone to ferry us while you do archery practice." He waves us on. "Choose targets that are at least the width of the canal away."

That's a long shot. Taji's arrow will never make it. Or Mikko's. It's tricky to shoot one-handed and even harder to hit a target you can't see. But Yoshi and Kyoko will have a chance, and I'll have no trouble. Archery has always been my strongest skill.

"There's nothing to aim at," complains Kyoko.

The land is as flat as ever, and the occasional tree is not waiting in the right place for us.

"You could go and stand over there," suggests Mikko. "That would give us a target."

Kyoko takes aim and lands a fist on Mikko's shoulder. "I'd be safe as long as you were shooting. You can't hit anything."

Ow. He rubs his arm. "That hurt. It's your fault now if I can't shoot straight."

Kyoko and Mikko always tease each other and often one of them ends up with a bruise. But their arguments never last long, and Kyoko is already rubbing salve into Mikko's arm.

"Would you like to share my bow?" I ask Mei.

She shakes her head. "I don't know how."

"I'll show you," volunteers Yoshi.

She shakes her head again, embarrassed. "I wouldn't be very good."

"You'll be fine," Taji says encouragingly. "I never hit anything."

"And Mikko hardly ever does, either," Kyoko adds.

"All right," Mei agrees reluctantly. "If no one laughs."

We can't really promise that. We laugh at each other all the time, but it doesn't matter. Laughter between friends never hurts.

Overhead, the clouds gather and the afternoon turns gray.

While we practice archery, Sensei bangs the gong. Before Mei has even had a turn, a barge appears in the middle of the canal.

"Ho, Captain," Sensei calls. "I require a passage to the other side."

The barge master pulls into the bank.

"I don't deal with foreigners." He scowls. "You can't trust them."

Mei edges closer to listen, and so do I.

"Do we look dangerous?" Sensei asks.

The question answers itself, and our master helps it along. "I'll make it worth your trouble," he promises.

"I'd have to take you in separate trips," says the barge master, avid eyes appraising our horses, our baggage, and us.

Is he calculating weight and space or how much our goods are worth if he pitches us overboard?

"He's the untrustworthy one," Mei whispers.

I agree. Especially when I spy an Eagle flag tied to a railing.

Sensei notices it, too. "I see you have had an important passenger."

"He came across the canal last month, heading west. This emblem was presented to me as a token of appreciation." The barge master beams.

But we know it is more than that. Qing-Shen left a message to make us fearful. *I am somewhere nearby. We will meet soon,* the flag sneers.

"It'll take me three crossings to ferry you all," the barge master decides.

His beady black eyes glitter like water-snake scales. Shifty and slippery. I bet lies slide easily from his lips.

But Sensei can chop a snake into bite-size pieces with his eyes closed. He is not concerned.

"Small groups will be fine," Sensei tells the barge master. "My name is Ki-Yaga. I am a teacher from Japan, and these are my students. We are on our way to study at the White Tiger Temple." He bows, a small bend in the middle. It's a message the barge master won't understand. But we do. Sensei has no respect for this man.

"Gather your arrows," Sensei calls to us. "The master will take us across."

Mikko and Kyoko race each other to collect the arrows.

"Your students can shoot a great distance," the barge master comments.

Sensei nods. "Far enough to pick the eye out of a man standing on a boat on the other side of the canal."

The message isn't lost on the barge master. He blinks nervously.

"Of course, I am not suggesting that will be necessary," continues Sensei. "Not with an upstanding and honest man such as yourself."

Chest puffed out, the barge master will take any compliment that comes his way, whether he's earned it or not.

"First, we must establish a trade," Sensei says. "I do not carry money."

The barge master's expression flickers. He can't steal what doesn't exist. Nor can he overcharge us when a price has been agreed.

"Will you accept this gong as payment for our passage?" asks Sensei.

Biting his lip, the barge master is unimpressed. "It looks like a flattened cooking pot."

"Things are not always what they seem," Sensei says. "But I can see you are a clever man. This was indeed once a pot that held rice and noodles."

The barge master inflates even more. About to burst, he looks like one of those spiky puffer fish the captain would often catch and throw back.

Sensei strikes the gong hard. Loud and commanding, it echoes up and down the canal. "Once a cooking pot, this was recently the funeral gong of a great sea captain. It guided him on his journey to the next world. It is a possession of power." Sensei's voice drops to a whisper. "Just as it called your barge to us, it will call many passengers to you."

There's money in that.

"I'll take it." The puffer fish snaps at the shiny bait.

Kyoko, Taji, and Yoshi travel first with two of the horses. Then Mikko and Mei with another two horses. Sensei and I wait with the last three.

With greedy eyes, the barge master helps us load them. No doubt he's plotting how easily he could overpower an old man and a boy with one leg.

Halfway across the canal, I feel the boat slow. Just a little. *Now we will have some fun,* the wizard whispers inside my head.

Swaggering, the barge master postures in front of Sensei. Arrogant and threatening.

"The White Tiger Temple has no friends around here. Not since the Imperial Palace turned against it. I bet I could get a nice reward if I made sure no samurai came to the temple's aid." He leans into Sensei's face. "I know all about the samurai and their swords for hire. How much is the abbot paying you?"

He knows nothing. A samurai fights for honor, not gold. And his sword is enough to ensure that any shrewd man keeps his distance. The barge master is a fool.

My teacher says nothing.

"I could push you overboard," the barge master boasts. "Then I would be three horses richer."

Sensei doesn't reach for his sword. He's not chopping snakes today. He's playing a different game.

"If you did that, my students' arrows would pierce your chest," Sensei says.

"The sun is in their eyes. The arrows would fall short," the barge master says, gloating. "You were right before. I am truly a clever man."

"Well, in that case, it would be a great waste of intelligence if my student ran his sword through your body."

Spinning, the barge master finds my blade leveled at his chest. I lean forward until the point touches.

"Ha-ha." The barge master laughs nervously, patting Sensei on the back. "It is a good joke we share, isn't it?"

His eyes are scared now.

I grin. Sensei laughs, too. "It is the most fun I have had in ages," he says. And he means it, except he and I are sharing a different joke from the barge master's.

On the other side, we unload and Sensei hands over the cooking pot gong and its soup-ladle mallet. The barge master doesn't deserve them, but it would take a lot to make Sensei break a promise.

Only Qing-Shen has ever done that.

Spinning, the barge master finds
my blade leveled at his chest.

CHAPTER SIX

礼

THE OTHER
VILLAGE

Rain falls in a mist, then drizzle. Finally, the sky rips open and the water pours down. Before, the drops tickled my face; now they slap and sting.

Three days pass by, soaking into each other as we follow the endless roll of the plain. There are more travelers on the road, but they don't speak to us. They pass by, their faces harried and downcast. "Good morning," we call in greeting. No answer. No one wants to talk to strangers.

I like the evenings best, when, saddle sore and weary, but with bellies full, we settle into our tent under the stars. To laugh and tease each other and listen to Sensei tell stories.

"My legs are numb," complains Mikko. "You're lucky you've only got one."

"I'm sure it's aching twice as much as yours," I moan. "Even my toes hurt."

"That's good." Sensei hands me a blanket. "Then you will sleep well."

Sensei finds something good in everything.

Despite the rain, it's not cold and the others curl up without any covers at all. But I like the weight of the blanket against my back. It's comfortable and safe.

Sometimes though, I wake in the middle of the night to see Yoshi sitting with the tent flap open, staring back across the plain. As if he can still see the ocean.

"What are you doing?" I asked the first time.

"Thinking," he said.

I dragged my blanket over and shared it with him so that Yoshi, too, would feel safe and comfortable. On the other nights I didn't even ask; I just wrapped my blanket around us both.

I reach down to massage some feeling back into my toes. Beside me, Taji does the same thing.

Sensei rustles in his bag, looking for the poultice of chain-fern bark he uses to help relieve our aches and pains. But there's no medicine for what ails Yoshi at night. The only cure is the morning. When we ride again.

"Can we stop at that village?" Mikko points to a clump of thatched roofs in the distance.

We've passed many villages, but each time, Sensei has said, as he does now, "It is not the right one."

"They're all the same to me," says Kyoko with sigh.

"Then it will not matter which one we stop at." Our master smiles.

Aha. I pounce. "But they are not all the same."

Yoshi strains to see. "How can you tell from this far away?" he asks.

"This village is very different. It is much closer than any other."

Sensei laughs, leaning against his horse's neck. "Then I am convinced. We will stop at the next village."

"I am looking forward to a meal made from something that's not dried black or smoked brown." Yoshi pats his stomach.

"I'll settle for a cushion to sit on." Taji grimaces.

"Somewhere out of the rain," adds Mikko, shaking his raincoat sleeve to spatter in my face.

Kyoko looks uncertain. "We might not even be welcome."

It's a good point. One I wish I had thought of myself.

"Few villages are friendly in these times," says Mei. "Perhaps we will be lucky when they see that I am not a foreigner."

The silence is filled with unease. There are only seven of us, and we have no allies on the plain. We are on our own. What if we're walking into danger? What if Qing-Shen is waiting for us here?

"Will we be welcome, Sensei?" Kyoko twists her hair around her littlest finger, the way she always does when she's worried.

Sensei shrugs. "Probably not, but it does not matter now that we have decided where we are going. A samurai does not change direction just because he is outnumbered."

"I'm not afraid," Mikko insists.

We raise our voices in support but not quite as loud as we normally would.

The path to the village is flanked by the now-familiar expanses of grain. Women and children pause from their planting to turn and stare. I try to hold their gaze, but, unnerved, I look away. The message passes from field to field. Strangers are coming. By the time we reach the first hut, the villagers are expecting us.

Men wait with surly faces and wary, distrustful eyes. Their pointed pikes are leveled at our horses' chests.

"Good choice of village, Niya," Mikko mutters.

"They would all be the same," Sensei says. "This is a time when an outlander must earn his welcome."

The first thing we earn is a push in the direction of a small bamboo-fenced enclosure. It's the sort normally used for horses or oxen, but today it also holds unwanted visitors. At least it has a roof, so we won't need raincoats anymore.

Our horses are allowed to graze unfettered, but our hands are tied together through the railings.

"What about this kid?" one man asks, unsure what to do with Mikko. "He's only got one hand."

"Then tie it up," snaps another.

"Not you," the man says as Mei puts her hands through the railing. "The chief wants to talk to you."

"And I've got a few words to say to him." Mei stands, hands on hips. The daughter of a village headman, she's used to being treated with respect. Mei belongs here on the plain. Only we are foreigners. Still, being different has never bothered us before. We've always been the odd ones out.

"What about their swords?" asks the villager.

"Leave them," sneers the man in charge. "They can't reach them."

Only a fool would leave a samurai anywhere near his sword.

The two men double-check each binding before taking Mei away with them. If Yoshi's eyes were daggers, both men would reel, clutching at the knives in their backs.

"What will happen now?" Kyoko asks.

"We will untie ourselves and wait until we are called. Then perhaps I will tell a story and we will be rewarded with a meal," says Sensei.

"We're not in any danger?" Mikko looks disappointed. After weeks at sea and days of riding, he's eager to swing his blade.

Sensei shakes his head. "Mei's father is a powerful man. He controls the sea trade inland to the smaller villages. When the chief discovers who Mei is, we will suddenly become honored guests. In the meantime, Kyoko will untie us."

I can't even move one hand. There's no way I could ever get my knots undone, but an extra finger provides extra reach. Kyoko is soon free and untying Sensei.

"It had better be a good lunch," Yoshi says grumpily, rubbing his wrists.

"The pre-dinner entertainment is already terrible," Taji complains as he returns his sword to his belt.

Poor Taji. All he wanted was a cushion to sit on, and

instead we're squirming on the hard ground, trying to find spaces between the duck droppings. It doesn't bother Sensei. He can sit cross-legged and comfortable on a mound of spiky grass.

Three men enter the enclosure. Eyes bright with mischief, their hands clasp pointed sticks. The threat lurks, raising its head just far enough to see us. Sensei is not concerned. Pretending to be still bound, we wait for trouble to show its hand.

Fingers creeping toward his scabbard, Mikko can barely contain his grin.

"What have we got here, cousin? It seems someone has captured a troop of great samurai warriors." A scrawny chicken-bone man waves his pike in mock swordplay.

"They don't look so high and mighty to me," his friend jeers.

"We do our best," Sensei says. "But often it is not what you see but what you don't see that is important."

The men are not paying attention.

"This one's a bit girlie," the third rogue says, tugging at Kyoko's topknot.

She grits her teeth. One sword stroke from her and

the man would have no hands. Fingers twitching, I'm eager to wield my blade for her. But our master's eyes say to wait, so neither of us moves.

"This kid only has one hand." The chicken man is surprised.

"You don't need two hands to cut off one head," Sensei teaches. But the class is not listening.

"This one only has one leg," says the second man.

"You only need one arm to swing a sword. No legs are necessary," Sensei persists.

"And this one," the third man says, snickering, "is blind."

"You do not need to see when your target is boorish and loud," our teacher says with a sigh.

"Are you insulting us?" The chicken man finally turns to Sensei.

His friend kicks straw at our master's sandals. "Silly old fool."

But these men are the foolish ones, and the pre-dinner entertainment is about to become much more exciting.

"In my younger days, I was a famous swordsman," Sensei says. "It's true that I am old now, but the wise man fears me even more."

The villagers' laughter gurgles in their throats as they find themselves surrounded by six sword tips.

"N-no offense intended," the chicken man stutters.

"Are you offended?" Mikko asks me, touching his sword against the man's chest.

"Yes, I think I am," I say. "What about you, Taji?"

Before Taji can answer, the village chief storms into the enclosure. Mei hurries behind him. "What's going on? Why are you men harassing my honored guests?"

"We were just demonstrating a few samurai sword skills," says Sensei. "These men were kind enough to show interest, and we have appreciated their company."

"I must speak with our visitors in private," the chief says, waving the men away. He turns to Sensei. "A terrible mistake has been made. Please accept my apology."

Sensei nods politely, but Mei interrupts. "In Japan, the depth of a man's bow is the extent of his apology," she says.

The headman takes the hint and knees bent, presses his nose to the duck-poo-splattered ground.

Mei winks, and even Sensei struggles not to laugh.

Upright, with his dignity restored, the headman takes charge. "Come, my new friends. We cannot feast

"N-no offense intended," the chicken
man stutters.

since the crops are poor, but we can still eat. If necessary, we can throw in a few grasshoppers." He laughs, and his big belly jiggles. Times might be hard, but he has not missed any meals recently.

"I'm not eating bugs," says Mikko.

Kyoko makes a face. "Yuck."

"You wanted fresh food," I murmur to Yoshi, who looks as green as he did the day our boat pitched and rolled in the storm.

"They are very crunchy and good for the sword arm," Mei says.

"Really?" asks Mikko. He takes swordsmanship seriously. Enough to eat a grasshopper.

"No." She giggles. "But they are very tasty. I've had them before."

"You don't eat cockroaches, do you?" Taji teases. His eyes can't see, but they smile all the time.

"Definitely not," says Mei. "Cockroaches are much too useful. Did you know you can use crushed cockroaches to make a poultice to heal bones and stop bleeding?"

"You can never have too many cockroaches," Yoshi agrees.

I like Mei. She would make a good Little Cockroach.

The meal is duck egg on rice. Warm and filling. Not a grasshopper in sight. Yoshi has a big grin across his face and one arm draped contentedly across his stomach.

While the chief calls for tea, I whisper in Sensei's ear, "Why did you protect those men after they insulted us?"

"Are you a lesser samurai for their words?" he asks.

"No."

"But they are much better men because of my words." He taps me gently on the side of my temple.

Now I have learned a lesson, too.

After sweet dumplings, the chief unbuttons his jacket and leans back on his cushion. His greedy eyes rest on Sensei's scabbard. "I see you are a swordsman."

Sensei nods. "I have won many duels in my own country."

"A samurai sword would be a fitting weapon for a village leader." The chief's eyes are calculating the risk. The sword would be a great prize. Maybe even worth risking Zhou's displeasure.

Sensei's unsheathed blade flashes like lightning. The speed of the draw and the gleam of its sharp edge are not lost on the chief. Our teacher's message is received and read. Much as the chief would like Sensei's sword, he knows he would not live to see it won. Twenty men might overpower our master, but by then the chief's head would be rolling across the floor.

"Perhaps you have heard of the Middle Kingdom's greatest warrior, Qing-Shen. He was here a month ago," the chief boasts. "I have heard he has returned to the plain, and I am hoping he will visit me again."

Untucking a silk square from his belt, the chief proudly waves it in front of Sensei's face. The Eagle flaps its wings to mock us. "I have heard Qing-Shen is extremely well trained in swordplay," says Sensei.

He certainly is. Especially if Sensei taught him all he knows.

"Qing-Shen moves like a leopard running with the wind. He leaps with a great roar," brags our host. "He is so fast, no one sees him. Only the rush of air tells of his passing."

I raise my eyebrows at Yoshi. No one is that good.

"I have also heard that his sword can be hired and that for the sake of money, he has done things no warrior should do," says Sensei.

"Ah, well." The chief chuckles. "We all have to eat,

and no hero is perfect." He nudges our teacher. "Not even a legendary warrior."

But Sensei is not amused. He would not trade his honor for a meal. Not for the best chow mein in all of China. Sensei would rather starve.

He rises to his feet. "Thank you for your hospitality. It is time for us to leave. Many days of travel still lie ahead of us," Sensei says. "We are expected at the White Tiger Temple."

"You will need to hurry." The chief laughs. "I have heard a rumor that it may not be there for much longer."

"We will take only one horse. I trust you to send the rest back to Zhou." Sensei's voice is cold and sharp like his sword. "If my friend does not receive them in five days, he will come to collect what he is owed."

It's a barely veiled threat. Sensei doesn't trust this man at all, and he doesn't like him, either.

I'm glad to leave the village behind even though we're sloshing though the rain. Our bamboo hats and raincoats keep us dry, and the air is still warm. It's much more comfortable here without the chief reminding us about Qing-Shen.

"I really wanted to sleep in a soft bed tonight," Taji moans as we settle into the familiar rhythm of walking.

"I thought you just wanted a cushion," teases Mei.

"I am aiming higher now that I am traveling with such an important man's daughter." He ducks as Mei reaches out to thump him.

"Tomorrow you will sleep in beds," says Sensei.

"Real beds?" Kyoko asks. "In a room with walls?"

"A day's walk away across the Yellow River is a large city. There I will learn exactly where Qing-Shen is and whether the road to the temple is still safe."

"Perhaps Qing-Shen will listen to reason and you won't need to fight," suggests Taji.

Looking at our master, I dare to hope. Sensei's words are even stronger than his sword.

"It is not possible," Sensei says. He looks sad. "Qing-Shen will never forget my broken promise or that I banished him from the Cockroach Ryu."

Why was Sensei looking for a replacement anyway? Surely he'll teach at our school forever. Sensei looks inside me all the time, but he is not listening in my head now. His mind is elsewhere.

"Is it a matter of honor?" Yoshi asks.

Honor is always a matter of life and death.

"It is a matter of greed. Qing-Shen wants the two things I promised. He wants my secret and my treasure."

"What treasure?" asks Kyoko.

Sensei has many secrets, but he certainly doesn't have any treasure. And two is definitely not a lucky number. Not even if all the people in China say so.

Our teacher passes the reins of Izuru to me and turns his staff upside down. Untwisting the base, he reaches inside and extracts a small rice-paper box. Like a ninja dagger sheath, Sensei's walking stick has a secret compartment at the bottom.

The box is bright red with gold embossed symbols. Removing the lid, Sensei lifts out a tiny perfect square of white jade.

Mikko whistles. "That must be worth a fortune."

And to think Sensei has been dragging it through the mud and tapping it in the dust for as long as we have known him.

"It is more precious than gold," Sensei agrees. "It can open the gates to the Forbidden City and even the door to the Emperor's chambers."

"It doesn't look like a key," I say.

Sensei laughs. "It is truly a master key. It will open any door, and I had to master half a million of Confucius's words to earn it."

Ha! Sensei *does* know Confucius after all. I grin at Mei, but she is looking at Sensei with new admiration.

"You were a finalist in an Imperial Exam," she exclaims.

It must have been a tough exam for Mei to be awed by a test result. Archery bulls-eyes and sword points are important, not marks on a piece of paper.

"Why would anyone come all the way to China just to take an exam?" Mikko shakes his head, confused. Mikko wouldn't even go as far as the room next door.

"It is a very prestigious exam," explains Sensei. "All over China, scholars compete to win a government position. There are many tests to pass before you reach the finals. The top candidates receive their certificates from the Emperor himself. This jade seal was given to me when I gained first place."

Even more impressed, Mei is open-mouthed. "A first-place candidate can marry a princess," she whispers.

"A princess?" muses Mikko. "Now *that* might inspire me to work hard."

"I doubt it," Kyoko says.

It's true, and anyway, Mikko's heart already belongs to my sister, Ayame. Mikko is a great swordsman, but my irritating little sister felled him without even drawing a blade. Girls, like the ninja, have secret powers. Even though Yoshi refuses to fight, he might just change his mind if it was about Mei. I've seen the way he looks at her when he thinks no one is watching.

"If I give this seal to another man, all its privileges are transferred," Sensei says. "And if another man kills me, this will be his."

"It would be a powerful weapon in Qing-Shen's hands." Taji traces his finger across the jade.

"Yes. He would wield it with the same lack of honor as he does his sword. I will never let *him* have it. Do you know what the symbol for the highest rank of government official is?" Sensei asks.

We don't, but Mei does. "It is the White Crane."

See, Sensei whispers inside my head. *You could be just like me.*

I grin and whisper back. *Or perhaps you are already just like me.*

Smiling, he nods. *It is the same thing.*

"How could anyone learn half a million words?" Mikko is amazed.

"I will tell you a secret," says Sensei, wringing the rain from his beard. "Wise words are the same wherever you go. Even across the sea. Confucius said, 'Wisdom, compassion, and courage are the three universally recognized moral qualities of men.'"

Sensei grins. "Does that sound familiar?"

"*Chi, jin, yu,*" we chorus.

The code of the samurai. Even Confucius knew it.

As we walk, our teacher and Mei swap favorite sayings. Soon we all know at least a hundred things Confucius said.

Sensei is in the mood for answering questions. So we fire as many as we can, whistling like arrows.

"Why has the Imperial Palace turned against the temple?" I ask.

"The balance of power in the palace is changing, and the new military leaders are afraid of the fighting monks of Shaolin. Some talk of burning the temple. The abbot has recalled some of his students from abroad to collect pieces of the temple for safekeeping."

"What piece will we be given?" wonders Taji.

Hmmm. Sensei is thoughtful. "The temple holds many valuable things. Books, statues, artifacts and stone buddhas."

"It all sounds heavy to carry," I say.

But Sensei will take whatever he is given. And we will carry whatever he asks. It'll be a slow journey. But then even Confucius had something to say about that. *It does not matter how slowly you go as long as you do not stop.*

CHAPTER SEVEN

勇

WHEN CHINA
CRIES

"Let's play a game," Mei says, wiping the rain from her chin.

Kyoko claps her hands in excitement.

"Excellent," says Sensei. He's walking ahead, leading my horse, but he still hears every word.

I think it's a good idea, too. Anything to distract us from the threat of Qing-Shen.

"Confucius says, 'Touch your nose.'" Mei places her finger on her nose and we copy her.

"Confucius says, 'Touch your feet.'"

"Niya's not doing it right," teases Kyoko. "He's only touching one foot."

If anyone else said that, I'd flatten them.

When friends laugh and tease you, it still feels good. I know my missing leg doesn't matter to *them*. When people say nothing or pretend they haven't even noticed what is right there under their nose, that's when you know it's a problem.

"Drop to the ground!" Mei yells.

We crouch into the mud.

She giggles.

"What?" Taji asks.

Mei laughs even more. "I didn't say, 'Confucius says.' You're all out."

And we deserve to be. It's all right to do something because Confucius said. He was old and wise, and even Sensei quotes him. But you'd have to be pretty silly to do something just because Mei said so.

Hmph. Sensei coughs to attract our attention. He's still standing, of course.

As we walk, we play more games. When the wind rises and the rain peppers my face, I don't mind. I'm having fun with my friends. If only Qing-Shen wasn't waiting to ruin everything. He sneaks into our thoughts all the time.

"I wonder where Qing-Shen is now," Yoshi says.

"Behind us, closing fast," replies Sensei.

"How do you know? I thought he was in front of us." I peer back along the direction we came. "Can you hear him coming?" I look at Taji, who shakes his head. If the Golden Bat can't hear anything, not even Sensei could.

"I don't have to hear. I taught him everything I know. And I know where I would be," our master says. "Sometimes in front and sometimes behind, Qing-Shen weaves backward and forward, always looking for the moment to pounce."

I try to imagine China's Warrior as a boy, just like

me. Whose bed did he sleep in at the Cockroach Ryu? I hope it wasn't mine. I was proud when I found out the great swordsman Mitsuka Manuyoto once slept in my bed, and I was even prouder when I met him. But if I ever found out Qing-Shen slept on my mattress, I would sleep on the floor for the rest of my school life.

One question won't let me go. Why would Sensei ever want to leave the *ryu*?

"Why did you want to train someone to replace you?" Taji asks my question.

"I have something I must eventually leave to do. When a man makes a mistake, he must go back and restore the balance. Otherwise he will never be free," Sensei says.

Nodding, Yoshi understands that. Many things have gone awry for him, too. But what went so wrong for Sensei?

I know he heard my unasked question, but he doesn't answer it. So aloud, I ask a different one. "Will it ever be right? Will it ever end?"

"Everything ends. We all die," Sensei says. "But I have a lot to do. I have many tasks still to complete, so I do not have time to die."

The determined look on Sensei's face convinces me that there's nothing to worry about. Yet.

The rain grows heavier, and beneath our sandals the path turns to muddy sludge. We meet many people, but they are all going in the opposite direction. No one is heading toward the river. They are all hurrying away.

"Turn back, Grandfather." One after another, they give Sensei the same advice.

Our teacher doesn't listen.

"Don't be a fool!" they yell. "The river is rising."

Sensei walks even faster toward it. He is not afraid of danger, but I'm nervous. If we rush to the temple, we might not make it there at all. "How will we get across the river, Master?" Mei asks. "There will be no ferryman waiting to carry us."

And after our last experience, I wouldn't trust one, anyway.

Sensei scratches his chin. "We will need a boat. I will ask to purchase one."

None of the people who pass us have a boat with them, but surely some will have left one moored behind.

"Do you have a boat to sell?" Sensei asks each group we pass. Many do, and our horse would easily cover the cost. But each time Sensei shakes his head. "No. That is not the boat I am looking for."

If he doesn't find it, we might have to swim. The path is now a deepening puddle.

"Master," an elderly man calls to Sensei, "please go back. You are going the wrong way."

The old woman beside him waves us to turn around, and the little girl holding her hand copies the motion.

Sensei shakes his head. "I must continue on. A man must follow the path he is given, and I have important business in Kaifeng."

"Is your business so urgent that it is worth risking your life and those of your students?"

"Yes, it is," says Sensei.

It must be something very important. Sensei doesn't value his own life, but he treasures ours.

Chewing on his bottom lip, the old man says nothing. He understands.

"How many days before the river is too swollen to cross?" Sensei asks.

The old one nods and blinks, using his face to count. Seven nods. "If it keeps raining like this, she'll probably only hold her banks for seven days."

"And then what?" Kyoko whispers.

"Then China will cry," Mei says. "Many lives will be lost. Farmers and their families will drown first. And if the walls of Kaifeng are breached, the streets will clog with floating bodies. It's happened before."

I hope Sensei finds the right boat soon. And I hope the riverbanks hold.

"If you must cross the river, take my boat," the man offers before Sensei has a chance to ask. "It is well worn and shabby, but it is a reliable vessel. I left it tied to a tree near my house."

Sensei takes the old man's hand in his own. "I have been searching for the right boat. And I will pay you well now that I have found it."

"No. No." The old man shakes his head. "The boat is no use to me, and you will need all the money you have in the streets of Kaifeng. It is not a safe place. Its people flee in panic. They say the barbarian army is advancing south, and anyone who looks out their window can see the threat of flood."

Beside him, his wife shakes her head, too, and the granddaughter mimics her, her wet hair flicking back and forth.

"I do not need money," Sensei says. "Which is a good thing, since I don't have any. But I do have this horse, which I cannot take any farther. If you accept her as payment, you would be doing me a great service."

"Thank you, Master. It is a generous offer." The old one bows. "This horse will make our journey much easier. When my wife is tired, she will be carried. And when my granddaughter cries, she can ride. Your horse is in good hands."

Sensei smiles. He already knows that.

The man gives us directions to his home. We wave until even the little girl is tired of waving back and drops her arm.

"Now we have the right boat," Sensei says.

"How do you know it is right when you haven't even seen it?" Mikko is as puzzled as I am.

"It does not matter what the boat is like," Sensei says. "The right boat is the one whose owner will best look after our horse."

I miss the *clop-clop* of Izuru beside us, but I knew we couldn't take her all the way to the temple and back. Our hearts are lighter knowing that a boat has been found and our horse will be safe. I flick dirty puddle water at Mikko, who returns a wave, washing a muddy ring around my ankle.

A deepening layer of rainwater now covers the low ground. With every step, it creeps farther up my leg. It won't be long before we need the boat.

But what if it's not there? I trust the old man, but what if someone has stolen it?

Inside my head, Sensei answers. *Who is there to steal a boat? Do you see anyone else walking in the direction of the river?*

No, I don't.

And it makes the White Crane nervous.

The boat is a cross between a small fishing vessel and a canal barge. Flat-bottomed but with a rudder to steer and oar poles to push it out into the deep water. Anchored to a thin sapling, the vessel strains against its fraying rope.

Together we empty the rainwater from the boat and drag it toward the river's edge, where sandbag levees raise the height of the bank. Directly across the river are the walls of Kaifeng. They loom, gray and forbidding. Threatening. Suddenly, I don't want to go there at all. I'm afraid of what we might find.

Fear is your friend, Sensei says. *It sharpens the mind.*

But right now I would rather be dull and safe.

"In Kaifeng, we must be careful," advises Sensei. "The threat of invasion makes strangers unwelcome. The soldiers on the gate will be suspicious of a group of foreigners."

With one last heave, we push the boat into the river.

"We will spend a night with an old friend of mine, Chu Ting." Our master gestures for us to load our packs into the vessel. "Once Chu Ting was a high-ranking general in the Chinese army, but now, like me, he is an old man. He is a good storyteller. Even more important, he is a great listener, and that trait has revealed many things to him. For as far as the crane flies, there is nothing the ex-general does not know. He will be able to tell me what lies ahead of us."

Sensei throws his pack on top of ours. "Not even Qing-Shen can hide from General Chu."

I try not to think about Qing-Shen, but I know that the closer we get to the temple on Song Shan, the closer we are to him. Somewhere on the other side of the river, he stands waiting, barring our way. Maybe he lurks in the streets of Kaifeng.

"A word of warning." Sensei laughs. "Don't mention clocks in front of General Chu."

"Why not?" Kyoko's eyes gleam with mischief. I can see she's tempted already.

"It is his great passion." Sensei rolls his eyes. "He can lecture for hours. Time passes very slowly when Chu Ting talks about it."

"Kaifeng was once the site of a great water clock," Mei says proudly. "It's gone now, destroyed by war. It only remains in the words of men like General Chu."

I shake my head. "I don't understand why anyone would want to count time. If I want to know what time it is, I look up at the sun."

"Hard to do today," Taji says with a laugh. Overhead, the sky is clouded and rain-sodden, the sun long chased away.

The boat rocks uneasily in the water. I feel uneasy, too. "What if one of us falls in the river?" Yoshi is worried now. He's probably remembering the night the captain died.

"If we fall in, we will swim," Sensei says.

He makes it sound so simple. But now it's Mei's turn to look worried. "Floodwater moves quickly, and it is freezing cold. Much colder than you would ever expect. No person could ever swim in it."

But maybe a Cockroach could. During winter, pieces of ice fleck the river below the *ryu,* but that doesn't get us out of swimming lessons.

"My students have been practicing cold-water swimming," says Sensei.

A samurai must be well prepared. And no one is better prepared than our master's students.

"I'm not a good swimmer," admits Mei.

Yoshi hesitates. He can feel the weight of the captain slipping away from his grasp. But he's not going to let that happen to Mei. No matter how fearful he is, Yoshi will never let his friends down.

"If we have to swim, I will carry you."

Mei is still unsure. "What if I sink?"

"If it makes you feel safer, I will hold your hand," Yoshi offers.

Kyoko giggles and Taji winks, poking Mikko and me in the ribs at the same time. Even Sensei curls his lip to hide a smile.

"Chop, chop, Little Cockroaches. It is time to go," says Sensei.

"Are you sure it's safe?" Mei looks nervously at the boat.

"No, I am not. But I am sure it must be done. The temple needs us. Confucius said, 'It does not matter how slowly you go . . .'"

"'. . . as long as you do not stop,'" I say.

Smart man, Confucius. Almost as wise as Sensei.

The sky grows even darker as the storm builds. Clouds race to crash into each other. It's not far across the river, but there's no time to waste. The world has turned deep gray-green, and Yoshi's face is painted the same color.

"Hurry, hurry!" Sensei calls as Yoshi helps Taji aboard. Kyoko scrambles in easily, and Mei takes Yoshi's hand with a smile even though I can see she doesn't need any help. Mikko's strong arm gives me a final push, almost enough to send me sprawling, except Yoshi steadies me. Getting on board is a team effort.

Mikko and I take one oar, Yoshi and the girls the other.

"Heave!" Sensei yells, and we throw our weight against the wind.

The boat is strong and solid, as the old man promised,

and today the Yellow River is our unexpected friend. The water rushes and surges, but it pushes in the direction we want to go.

Standing on the bow, Sensei raises his staff into the pouring rain as we forge our way through the foam to the other side.

Thunder splits the sky, and the rain falls in great chunks to churn the river to froth. The boat dips forward.

"Drop!" Sensei yells.

And without question we do. We've played this game in practice so many times before. "Flat against the deck," he calls again.

We spread like the rock lizard, trying to absorb the pitch of the waves. Minutes crawl, itching across my back. I want to scratch, but I'm too frightened to raise even one hand. If I stay still, I'm glued safely in place.

Finally, Sensei sets us free.

"You can get up now."

The water surges beneath our hull, but the boat is steady. Oars driving, we push on through the turbulence toward the other side.

Lightning swipes and thunder hammers. Suddenly, the Dragon rears its head to demand the river toll. A great wave rises, hanging over the prow of our boat. Its watery scales reach out to coil around Sensei's thin waist, knocking the staff from his hands.

The staff skids across the deck, smacking hard against my leg. I collapse in pain, watching helplessly as Sensei is dragged from the boat.

Mei screams.

"No-o-o!" Yoshi bellows.

Last week's nightmare wakes to swallow us all over again.

White-faced, Taji grips the side of the boat. Mikko is frozen still, and Kyoko crumples beside me, sobbing.

"Go on without me," Sensei calls, his voice fading.

Frantically, we scan the waves, looking for where the voice came from, willing our master to speak again. Panic-driven, the White Crane searches. It soars above the river, screeching in pain.

But our master is nowhere to be seen. The toll has been paid.

Do not be afraid. I will meet you at the temple, Sensei whispers. *Tell the others.*

When I repeat his words, my friends look into the darkness. Uncertain. They desperately want to believe.

Suddenly, the dragon rears its head
to demand the river toll.

"Are you sure?" Taji asks. "I didn't hear anything."

I hesitate. If the Golden Bat didn't hear anything, maybe I imagined it. Our teacher must have sunk straight to the bottom.

Tell me again, I call to Sensei inside my head.

But there's no answer.

"Are you sure?" Kyoko repeats Taji's question.

Miserably, I shake my head. When China cries, I do, too.

CHAPTER EIGHT

真

THE WALLED
CITY

We tie our boat to a tree and huddle together, heads bowed, hearts numb. Rain drips from our bamboo hats to pool in our sandals.

"Perhaps we should turn back," Mikko says finally.

Taji shakes his head. "We would never make it back across the swollen river."

"And we would be less welcome than ever now. There are already too many extra mouths to feed on the plain," Mei adds.

Kyoko turns to face the river. "I want to go home."

But home wouldn't make us feel any better. Sensei is not there.

Yoshi says nothing. Sensei is gone with the river, and Yoshi has grown small again. We complain about our master all the time, but without him, we feel incomplete. Sensei's teachings make us whole.

"We have to go on," I say, holding our master's staff against my chest. It brings me comfort, but it also brings responsibility. "We have to honor Sensei's commitment."

"The White Tiger Temple still needs our help," Taji agrees. "It will make me feel better to know I am completing the task our teacher began."

Mei nods. "It is said that you cannot prevent the Bird of Sorrow from flying over your head, but you can prevent it from nesting in your hair."

Sensei would have agreed with that. But our problem now is that the Bird of Sorrow wants to nest in our hearts.

Inside me, the White Crane shakes its long neck, ready to peck and protect. There is only room for one bird in my heart.

I raise Sensei's staff, and all eyes follow. "Let's go." I point toward the walls of Kaifeng.

One step after another, we force ourselves forward.

"I hate the water." Yoshi spits the words.

Gently, Mei puts her arm around his waist to comfort him. She seems to know exactly what to say, and I'm glad to leave my friend in her hands. Perhaps Mei can show Yoshi how to close the lid on this new box.

"Do you feel left out?" Kyoko asks me, glancing toward Yoshi and Mei, leaning against each other.

"No." I smile. "I am glad of anything that helps Yoshi." And it's especially easy to understand with Kyoko here beside me. Girls can make you feel strange sometimes. They can turn your brain to porridge with a word, then raise your heart on colored kite strings with another. Right now Yoshi's heart needs to soar. To somehow rise above the pain of Sensei's disappearance and the loss of our captain.

Wandering the perimeter of the city walls, we count the guards. At least four on the front gate and others scattered at posts in between. This is a city on alert for the retreating army and the rumor of barbarians from the north.

"Fools." Mei clicks her tongue. "They should be watching the water. More people in this city have died from floods than any battle."

"It must be an awful way to die," says Kyoko.

In the silence I'm sure we're all thinking the same thing. Sensei at the bottom of the river, Captain Oong under the waves.

Mikko places his hand on his sword for reassurance. "I'd much rather die in combat. There is no honor in drowning."

"And you know what?" I wave the staff excitedly

through the air as if it is a sword. "I don't think Sensei has drowned. He would never die without honor."

"Are you sure?" Taji asks.

"No, but I am hopeful. I hope Sensei is alive and waiting for us at the temple."

A calm settles on our shoulders, like the hand of an old friend. Or a teacher. Even if Sensei is no longer with us, we know what we have to do. And even if our hearts are full of sadness, we can still make a little room for hope.

My spirit is exhausted, and my body is dead tired.

"We should get some rest," I say. "But first, we need a plan."

I look to Yoshi for help.

He takes a deep breath, then finally speaks. "Nightfall is our best opportunity. We could pretend we are an escort for Mei. In these times, the daughter of a village chief would need protection traveling across the plain. A band of foreigners is better than none."

His voice is strong and sure. It's a good sign all around. Yoshi's confidence is returning, and the plan sounds like it will work. Settling with our backs against the wall, we share the remaining egg rolls from Sensei's pack while we wait for evening to come. Clutching the staff, I close my eyes and lean back into the last daylight hours.

A black crow caws through my sleep. It swoops toward the horizon. Uncurling its wings, the White Crane rises to follow. But someone wakes me before I reach the sky.

"Niya," Kyoko calls. "It's time."

"Was there a crow?" I mumble, dragging myself from sleep. "It's too dark to see, but I'm sure I heard one." I look at Taji, who shakes his head. I must have been dreaming.

Mikko rolls his eyes. "Surely you're not going to try to convince us again that Sensei is a *tengu*."

"Maybe I will," I tease. I'll say anything to lift my friends' spirits. If it helps Mikko to laugh at me, then I don't mind.

He sends a flying kick in my direction. Just close enough to make me flinch.

Sensei teaches us stick training, but Mikko hates it. He thinks the stick is a poor substitute for a sword. But Sensei's staff is a very powerful stick, and I thread it between Mikko's ankles to send him sprawling.

"I wouldn't mind if Sensei was a *tengu*," whispers Kyoko. "If it meant he was here with us."

"He's not here," I say. "But if we complete his mission, his spirit lives."

"State your business," the guard challenges.

"I am Mei-Ying, daughter of Chief Chen Zhou, whose village stands on the eastern edge of the Northern Plain."

"Never heard of him," snaps the guard.

"I am sure you have heard of Ex-General Chu Ting. I am his wife's new maid. I am required to report to the household by dusk, and already I am late. Could you tell me where the ex-general lives?"

"His home is a block to the left. You cannot miss it. A large pot of bamboo and two stone lions mark the entrance." The guard's eyes narrow. "It's very dangerous for a young girl to be out after dark. Perhaps I should detain your companions and accompany you myself."

There's a threat in the soldier's voice, and beside me

"State your business," the guard challenges.

Yoshi's hand moves for his sword. The soldier doesn't know it, but *he* is in the greatest danger of all.

"The ex-general would not be pleased if anything happened to his newest staff member. He has already paid one year's salary to my father." Mei's voice is soft, but her meaning is loud and clear.

"I wouldn't waste my time," sneers the guard. "Especially as you already have your own escort." Smirking, he turns his attention to us. "What strange manner of soldiers are *you?*"

"We are samurai." Mikko's voice booms with pride.

"Then I have been expecting you, although you are not quite as I imagined. You are much shorter and dirtier. Not glorious at all." The guard laughs. "Still, I have a message for you. For the one called Ki-Yaga."

"Our master is not with us," says Yoshi, ignoring the insult. "I will take the message for him."

The guard searches through his jacket and produces a small square of silk with an Eagle symbol in its center. My stomach lurches in recognition. Qing-Shen is still ahead of us. Waiting.

But he might have to wait a very long time. We don't even know whether Sensei is still alive.

"Thank you," Yoshi says. "When was this message delivered?"

The guard scratches his head, then his chin and his head again. "A few days ago at most." He stares, his brow furrowed, perhaps deciding whether to interrogate us further.

"May we go now? The ex-general will be growing impatient," Yoshi reminds him.

Waving us through, the guard turns his attention to the flask he found in his pocket.

"We're being followed," Taji whispers.

I can't hear anything, but I would never question Taji's ears.

There are only three reasons anyone would follow us: to spy, to steal, or to kill. Our shoddy clothes and thin muddy packs wouldn't interest the poorest band of robbers. A lone man might be tempted, except there are six of us and Yoshi casts a big shadow.

We walk slowly, dragging our steps to stretch the minutes. But nothing happens. Our pursuer must be a spy. And except for Taji's ears, he would be safe. We would never have known he was there.

There's only one person it could be. Only one person could sneak up so close to a group of ninja-trained samurai.

"It must be Qing-Shen," Yoshi says. "Perhaps he knows his message has been received."

"He'll probably lose interest when he finds out Sensei is not with us," suggests Taji.

Yoshi shakes his head. "No. He'll want information. He'll try to find out everything he can."

"Then let's give him information," I whisper. "The things we want him to know. If Sensei is still alive, it would help him if we distract Qing-Shen with false information." After a pause, I moan, "Poor Sensei," much louder this time. "He was not a good swimmer, and the Yellow River current was too strong."

Taji catches on first. "I knew Sensei would never die by the sword. There is no one good enough. But even he could not defeat the river in flood."

Kyoko starts to cry, and Mei joins in.

"What will we do?" Mikko wails.

"We must continue on," Yoshi says. "Hush, now, or you will wake the townspeople."

Taji points down a street to the right. We weave around in squares, doubling back to lead our follower on a wild crane chase.

"He's gone," Taji whispers.

If Qing-Shen thinks our teacher is dead, then perhaps he'll stop tracking him.

There's only one house guarded by lions and potted plants. Kyoko gasps. Tied to a stalk of bamboo is another Eagle flag.

"It might be a trap," says Mikko.

"We have to go in," Yoshi decides. "The ex-general might need our help."

I rap Sensei's staff at the entrance.

"We are Ki-Yaga's students," I tell the big man who opens the door.

"Welcome, twice welcome." He offers his arm to help me inside.

Finally, two is a lucky number. As long as Qing-Shen is not hiding inside.

Once I would have pushed the ex-general away, rejecting his gesture of pity. But now I am much wiser. He just wants to help. He's being polite, and I am the one being bad mannered if I refuse.

"Where is your master?" he asks.

"Sensei has gone before us," I answer.

"He told us to call here on our way to the White Tiger Temple," adds Yoshi. "He said you could advise us about the road ahead."

We don't tell General Chu everything. Not yet. Once Sensei trusted him, but times change. Sensei would starve rather than compromise his honor and Qing-Shen would sell his for a case of rice wine. But there are many shades in between. Who knows what this man might do in hard times?

Especially when he has many mouths to feed. We are surrounded by children of all ages and sizes.

General Chu scratches his gray-speckled chin. "Ki-Yaga always has a plan, and I am honored to provide whatever assistance I can. Your master is a wise man. Did you know he placed first in the Imperial Examinations? He knows all of Confucius's sayings, and Confucius said a lot."

"Except 'drop to the ground,'" I murmur.

My friends laugh.

"What is the joke?" General Chu asks. "I like a good Confucius joke."

I explain about the game we played with Mei and how she tricked us.

"So you like games?" The ex-general's eyes gleam. "Some entertainment before business is always a good idea."

Kyoko nods enthusiastically. She likes games best of all. And the ex-general is right. A little rest and relaxation is just the diversion we need right now.

"You will be very happy here," he says. "I have many games and many grandchildren waiting to play them."

The children jostle around us, their faces full of questions and curiosity. They tug Kyoko's hair and sneak forward to touch our scabbards.

"What happened to your leg?" a little girl asks.

"Shh," Mrs. Chu hushes. "You must not be rude."

"It's all right," I say, encouraging the girl to sit beside me. "I was born like this."

"Does it hurt?" She edges closer.

"Oh, no. And in Japan I am a champion hopper."

My new fan looks at me with admiration.

"Play a game with us. Please." A boy pulls a casket of dominoes from under a table.

Yoshi's eyes light up. I think dominoes is fun, but

for Yoshi, it is a test of strategy. Already, I can see the Tiger itching to try its claws against China's esteemed general.

We play lots of games.

"Again," a little one cries every time we finish. There is an endless line of grandchildren, but there are only so many games a samurai kid can play.

"Maybe later." Kyoko packs the cards back into their container.

"I hear you are a clock historian," Taji says to the ex-general.

"No, no," the little ones chorus. "Clock stories are boring. Tell us about the Great Wall."

"Yes, please do," says Mei.

Kyoko presses her hands together with delight. "We would be most honored, General."

No man can refuse those two smiles. Even a great soldier like General Chu is easily outmaneuvered by them.

He laughs. "You do not need to call me General. That was a long time ago."

"You have earned the title," I say. "In Japan your name is known. Ki-Yaga mentions it all the time."

It's sort of true. Earlier today Sensei talked about the ex-general a lot. Probably preparing us for this evening.

Beaming proudly, General Chu settles back into his chair and kicks off his sandals. Mrs. Chu brings his pipe and slippers. The grandchildren settle cross-legged around his feet, making space for us to sit with them.

"The Great Wall of China is really many small pieces not quite joined together. In places it snakes along the Dragon's back like a giant column of stone. In other areas, the spine is broken where the wall is falling down. Sometimes there is even a gap. But great things are made by melding the right pieces together, and it does not matter if a bit is missing."

We know that. Together my friends and I make a strong team. A missing arm or leg makes no difference at all.

"But how can a gap keep out an invader?" Yoshi asks.

General Chu sits up straight and pulls at his beard, just as Sensei does. It's a perfect mimic. "Just because you cannot see something does not mean it is not there."

Sensei says that all the time. But now, in my mind, it has another message. A more shadowy, sinister one.

I unfold the Eagle flag and Yoshi takes the silk square from his jacket. "Just because we cannot see Qing-Shen does not mean he's not still there," I say.

"Ah . . ." General Chu sighs. "China's thorn in Ki-Yaga's side. Where did you get those?"

"The guard at the gate gave us the silk, and the flag was tied at your doorway."

General Chu laughs. "Qing-Shen always had a dramatic streak. Sometimes I think he would have made an excellent actor in the theater if he wasn't such a good soldier."

"Can he be defeated?" Yoshi asks. Chu is a military man, expert at calculating odds.

"Any man can be overcome. Especially he who thinks he can't. Qing-Shen is an excellent swordsman. An expert with knives and explosives. He can hide in broad daylight and shoot an arrow through the knothole in a tree. Your master taught him well. But every warrior has a weakness. You must find his weakness."

"It is the same as every opponent we face," I say. "He underestimates us."

General Chu scratches his ear. "You must learn to look through his eyes to see if you are right."

I shake my head emphatically. "There's no way I want to be like Qing-Shen."

Taji laughs. "I look through the eyes of others every day, otherwise I would never see anything. But it doesn't make me a different person. I am not them."

He's right. And I don't have to do anything anyway. Taji is the one to look through Qing-Shen's eyes.

I smile. "When the time comes, you will be ready for the task."

"I don't want to fight anyone," Yoshi says abruptly.

Leaning forward, General Chu studies Yoshi's face.

Can he see the cracks where the pot is newly mended?

"Excellent. A good general never wants anyone to fight. Not himself or his men. But sometimes he must make a sacrifice for the sake of others."

"I'll find another way," insists Yoshi.

"Even better," says General Chu.

He stares into Yoshi's face again, and I can tell he likes what he sees. This man has earned our trust.

"Sensei fell into the Yellow River. He might be dead," I blurt out. "Then Qing-Shen won't be a problem anymore. Our master said Qing-Shen was only interested in revenge."

"If only we knew whether Sensei is still alive." Mikko sighs.

"What do you feel?" General Chu asks us.

Just because you cannot see . . . The words spin through my brain.

"I think he lives," I insist.

My friends nod, not quite so sure.

"Even if Sensei is dead, we are continuing on," says Yoshi. "We will answer the temple's call on our teacher's behalf."

"Then you will need to be aware that the road to the temple is dangerous. Every day there are reports of robbery and attack. The temple itself is still safe, and I suspect it will be for many months."

"How do you know all this?" Taji asks.

"I am told I am a good listener," General Chu says.

Mrs. Chu appears at her husband's elbow. "You are a good talker." She laughs. "These children have done enough listening. I think it is time for our travelers to get some rest. They still have a long way to walk tomorrow."

"Quite right. Everyone to bed." When General Chu commands, the troops rush to obey.

Mrs. Chu leads us to a large room at the far end of

the house. "This was once the servants' quarters, but they have all left. It is comfortable but sparse," she says apologetically.

"After riding a horse for days, walking through mud, and sleeping outside, this room is a great luxury," Mikko assures her.

"Why do you stay when everyone else is leaving?" Mei asks. "Soon the city will be empty. Surely General Chu is welcome throughout the Middle Kingdom."

Mrs. Chu places extra blankets on the end of each bed. "A city is not empty when it is your home and your family is there with you. Then it is a place filled with important people."

As this room is now. If only Sensei were here, too. Then it would be complete.

CHAPTER NINE

仁

GOLDEN EAGLE

"Five hundred years ago, Kaifeng was a great and powerful city. It is one of our most ancient capitals," says Mei, looking back toward the gray walls. "Once the pride of the Middle Kingdom."

It's nothing to be proud of now. A maze of streets pocked with missing paving stones, lined with run-down houses and moldy shopfronts.

"I enjoyed sleeping with a pillow," sighs Mikko.

"I liked having a roof over my head," Kyoko says. "Especially when it's raining."

I agree. The home of General Chu was warm, dry, and welcoming. I miss the soft beds almost as much as Mikko does. But I couldn't sleep in peace. My dreams were crowded with wet shadows and the dark specter of Qing-Shen.

"The edge of the river is a foolish place to build a city," Taji says. "I couldn't live somewhere like that, not knowing when my bed might float away. I would never get any sleep."

I didn't anyway. All night it rained through my head. No wonder I can't hear Sensei talking in there anymore. It's far too soggy.

"You could always hang by your toes from a rafter," Kyoko teases Taji.

Our Golden Bat can sleep anywhere. Just like our master. Perhaps that's why Sensei isn't reaching out to me. He's fast asleep, waiting for us to find him.

"We should get a good start while the weather is fine," I say. "General Chu said the road is dangerous. We don't want to be traveling after dark."

"Whatever happens, Sensei will be proud of us," Mei says.

"Nothing will happen," Yoshi insists. "I won't let it."

General Chu's words have worked their magic, and Yoshi is our leader once more.

The rain has stopped now, but it won't be long before it falls again. Here beside the Yellow River, the rain follows the plum season, and the plums were still ripe on the trees in General Chu's courtyard.

As we head toward the slopes of Song Shan, the scattered trees clump together. By midmorning, Taji's wish has been granted, and we are walking in the mountains.

"Owww," Mikko yelps as Kyoko pokes him with a cypress pine needle.

"Shhh," Taji hisses. "We're being followed again."

The footsteps are not soft this time. We can hear them

easily, now that Taji has pointed our ears in the right direction. It's definitely not Qing-Shen. These predators don't slither silently; they clomp like a herd of water buffalo. To brigands on the road, six kids traveling alone must look like an easy target.

"How many men?" Yoshi is already calculating and planning.

Taji places his ear against the ground, letting the earth answer.

"Five," he says.

It's Sensei's favorite number. Somewhere, I'm sure he's smiling.

"What should we do?" Kyoko asks.

They all turn to me for guidance. It's my responsibility as long as I carry Sensei's staff.

What would our master do? Even without his words inside my head, I have hours of lessons etched in my brain.

"A samurai must always be prepared," I announce.

Yoshi nods, understanding. He knows how to lead from here.

"There are six of us and five of them," he says. "They are bigger and stronger. But we are much smarter."

"And our swords are much sharper," adds Mikko.

Surprise is our other weapon. No one expects a one-armed boy to be a master swordsman. No man thinks a girl can hurt him. And no one ever believes a one-legged boy can stay upright long enough to cause any trouble. These cutthroats are about to find out just how hard a cockroach can bite.

"Kyoko, climb the tree and have your *shuriken* stars ready." Yoshi gives orders like a seasoned battle commander. General Chu would be impressed. "Niya and Mikko, sit with the packs. Make sure our assailants can see that you will be easy to overcome in a fight."

Yoshi laughs. It's a good joke. We know one arm and one leg don't make us easy at all. They give us a huge advantage.

"Taji, you sit over here with Mei."

We settle into our positions. Time takes forever to pass. It crawls and dawdles. No wonder General Chu is so fond of clocks. They force time to march in rhythm, and any good general would see the advantage in that. We wait patiently. The slowest swordsman always moves first, Sensei taught us.

The approaching men are big, noisy, and smelly. They saunter and swagger as if they own the road.

"Ho, ho, young travelers," the leader calls. His voice is honey-friendly, but I'm not fooled. A bee can have a nasty sting in its tail.

Small eyes gleam. His teeth are yellow and dirty. A greasy mustache droops from his top lip, and his lopsided smile is not to be trusted.

"Where are your friends?" he asks.

"What friends?" I try to look as vague as possible. "As we drew near, I counted six kids, and there are two spare packs on the ground. Where did the others go?" He turns to Taji.

"How would I know?" Taji points to his blind eyes. "I didn't see anything."

"What about you? What have you got to say?" The man points to Mikko, who exaggerates a one-armed shrug.

"I'll tell you." Mei stands. "The others took everything of value and left us here. Apparently, we were too slow for them."

"You'll be sorry if you're not telling the truth," the leader threatens, sidling up to Mei so close that she could spit on his cheek if she wanted to. I bet Kyoko would. But Mei is more patient. She knows she has him right where we want him to be.

But the brigand has a good point. We should tell the truth. It's the best way to hide something.

"Some people believe this rod contains a great treasure when wielded by the right hand," I say, brandishing Sensei's staff. "It is my most valuable possession."

The man laughs. "I have no need of a crutch, and if I was looking for a fighting *bo,* then . . ." He gestures to his men and the staves they carry. "What we have is already superior to that scrawny stick of bamboo."

Foolish man. Bamboo is hollow, and who knows what it might contain. But his thoughts don't travel that far. He's too busy laughing at me.

The leader's eyes narrow. "If you have nothing of value, then we'll have to take your weapons and sandals." He gestures to his companions to gather up our shoes and scabbards.

It's not a good move. The penalty for touching a samurai sword is death.

"One step closer, and I will slice you up to look like me," Mikko threatens, unsheathing his sword. Taji and I stand beside him, and three of the brigands hurry to line against us. One has a Chinese broadsword, one a short dagger, and the third a sharpened wooden pike. Lethal weapons in a trained hand yet no match for a samurai sword.

It doesn't matter because this is Yoshi's battle plan. No fighting allowed.

We stagger back, and our opponents rush forward, eager to exploit our fear. But samurai kids are not afraid of roadside robbers. We're just good actors. When Mei gives the signal, we lower our blades.

Whoosh. Swoosh. Kyoko's *shuriken* stars slice along the line, knocking the broadsword, dagger, and pike to the ground. Before our opponents can react, we've kicked their weapons away for Mei to collect. Our sword points press hard against their chests.

The remaining two bandits rush to help their comrades.

Ooomph. Yoshi drops from a tree. He won't swing his blade in a fight, but he has no qualms flattening his target with a great weight. Kyoko jumps, too. Her victim carries a lighter load as he flails to the ground. But he crumples yelping. Our Snow Monkey's claws are pine-needle sharp.

Soon all five are tightly bound.

"Let's find out what they know," says Taji.

Information surely passes quickly among thieves who share the road and its spoils.

"Tell us what you know about Qing-Shen," Yoshi demands, towering over the leader.

"Qing-Shen is faster than the wind. He comes and goes with the night breeze. He hides in thin air," the brigand leader says.

"He leaps like a panther and flies like an eagle," adds another.

And he's got the whole country fooled. No one is that good. Not even Sensei.

"Rubbish," interrupts Mikko, pinning his sword under the leader's nose. "Tell us where he is, or I'll shave the mustache from your face."

The man looks at Yoshi, who shrugs.

"You better tell Mikko," I suggest. "He made quite a mess of the last man he tried to shave."

Mikko draws his sword gently across the man's cheek, and a thin thread of blood forms. It drops onto the man's hand. It's easy to draw blood from the face with a shallow wound, but this man and his friends don't know that. Frightened, the leader begins to talk fast.

"It is said that Qing-Shen has left his troops at the

Great Wall. They say he has personal business to attend to in Kaifeng and he is in a hurry. The Emperor has given him a leave of absence."

"How long ago?" Yoshi asks.

"Maybe five days."

"Who else knows something?" Mei fixes her gaze on the brigand Yoshi flattened.

"They say Qing-Shen has gone hunting."

They're right. China's Warrior is hunting our teacher.

Suddenly, everyone has something to say, singing the praises of their hero.

"Qing-Shen is a master of the five animal forms. He pounces like the leopard. He soars like the crane and swipes like the dragon."

"He roars like the tiger and wriggles like the snake."

That doesn't worry me. Between us, we've got six animal forms. And when it comes to roaring and soaring, Yoshi and I are experts.

"Why are you so interested in Qing-Shen?" the leader asks, suspicious.

"I hear we are heading in the same direction. Perhaps

our paths will cross." Yoshi turns his back on the captives. "Let's go." He waves us up the mountain.

"Hey," calls the leader. "We answered all your questions. Aren't you going to untie these ropes?"

"No," Yoshi says.

"Don't you trust us?" another brigand asks.

"No," echoes Mei.

"I hope Qing-Shen murders the lot of you," the leader snarls. "He's not a man, you know. He is a golden eagle, a great winged dragon."

"And not even a *normal* samurai kid would stand against a dragon," another rogue sneers.

Maybe not. But a Little Cockroach can. We've done it before, and we've got a trophy to prove it. Dragons are strong and powerful, but there is nothing in heaven or on earth that's harder to kill than a cockroach.

We walk quickly and are soon beyond the tirade of insults.

The quiet green of the forest reminds us of home. Except for the occasional pilgrim coming down the mountain, the path is ours alone.

"Hold on. Wait for me," hails a voice from behind.

The man soon catches up. We're not slow, but we're

tired after many days of traveling. The leather on the bottom of our sandals grows thin, and every last mile feels twice as hard.

"Are you on your way to the White Tiger Temple?" the farmer asks. "Many strangers have been heading that way this last month."

He's wearing a wide-brimmed bamboo hat, the sort local villagers wear in the fields. Two bundles swing from a pole on his back. His face is swathed ninja-like in thick bandages, one colored with seeping blood. Through the slit in the bandages his eyes twinkle, friendly and honest.

"What happened to your face?" Kyoko asks.

"I was beaten by a group of ruffians on the road. They set fire to my hair."

Mei gasps.

That must have been very painful. Once I burned my hand on a pot of boiling rice. After, the skin blistered and peeled until my fingers bled.

The farmer sighs. "I went to the monks at the temple for help. They bandaged my face so it would heal and others would not have to look while it did. It is red and ugly."

"Are you on your way to the White Tiger Temple?" the farmer asks.

"How awful." Kyoko's eyes are wet with tears. Our Snow Monkey has a hard fist but a soft heart. If he wasn't a stranger, I'm sure she would hug him.

"How could they beat you?" Mei asks. "You don't even carry a weapon."

Our new friend's laugh is warm and contagious. "I have my aged grandfather here." He lifts his traveling staff high. "It might be old and thin, but it still taught a little respect to a number of young heads before I was overpowered."

Sensei would like this farmer a lot.

"But I notice I am not the only one who is handy with a weapon. I saw a group of bandits bound and tied farther back along the road. Am I right to guess that was your doing?"

"Yes," I say. The White Crane puffs its chest proudly. "They attacked us. They thought we were an easy target."

Impressed, the farmer nods to Yoshi. "I wager you are strong enough to defeat at least three of those bandits single-handedly."

Yoshi shakes his head. "I don't fight. I can't."

Everyone always asks why. But not the farmer. He nods respectfully.

"So, you're a swordsman," he says to me. "I've heard that the Japanese sword is the master of all blades and that only a great samurai can wield one. May I see your weapon?"

Reluctantly, I pass him my blade. It would be rude to refuse but without my sword, I feel naked and vulnerable. The White Crane shivers.

"What's wrong, Niya?" Kyoko asks.

"Nothing," I mumble, confused. Suddenly, I am cold and in a hurry to reach the temple. Maybe Sensei is there. Maybe he is in danger.

"Thank you," the farmer says, returning my sword. "It is indeed a most superior weapon."

I smile. What would a farmer know? His staff is solid and honorable but does not compare to one of Master Onaku's blades.

The farmer points to Sensei's staff. "Like me, you also have a good stout walking stick to protect you."

I shiver again and Kyoko lightly touches my hand.

"I'm all right," I say.

"We are students on our way to meet with the Shaolin abbot. We are hoping he will choose to instruct us," Yoshi tells the farmer. "Are you heading in the same direction?"

"No. Not this time. I work in a village to the east. About a day away. I am returning home from a trading visit to another village." He points to the bags on his pole. "It is unusual to see students on the road without their teacher."

"Our teacher had a terrible accident," says Mikko.

"He is no longer with us." Taji's voice is sad.

I shudder again. The White Crane screeches in fear as a cold shadow passes through my heart. Has something dreadful happened? We need to get to the temple. Now.

"I am sorry, but we have to hurry. You are welcome to continue on with us, but we have to walk much faster," I say to the farmer.

"Is something wrong?" he asks.

My friends look at me with eyes that repeat the same question.

"I don't know," I answer.

"Then I will wish you good speed. I must leave the road here. Till we meet again." He tips his hat and melts into the trees.

As if he was never there at all.

As if he floated on the wind.

"Where did he go?" Mei peers into the forest.

The White Crane shrieks a warning. *Qing-Shen is faster than the wind. He comes and goes with the night breeze. He hides in thin air.*

"You know who I think that was?" I whisper.

"Oh, no." Mikko laughs and my friends join in. "Not again. You think Sensei is a *tengu* and some old farmer is Qing-Shen. And in Toyozawa you thought an old tramp was . . ."

They stop laughing. The tramp was the famous swordsman Mitsuka Manuyoto.

And the farmer *was* Qing-Shen.

"But he seemed so nice," Kyoko moans. "I am such an idiot. He misled me completely." She kicks at the ground.

"It's nothing to be ashamed of," I say. "He fooled Sensei, too, remember."

"But you worked it out. You deserve to carry Sensei's staff," Mikko says.

Yoshi is not bothered. "This is excellent," he says.

"What do you mean?" asks Mikko. "Qing-Shen just found out all about us. He even examined Niya's sword."

"General Chu told us we need to know our enemy.

And now we do. I saw how he handled a sword, how he moved his feet to balance its weight. I learned about him as much as he learned about me. Although I, too, am embarrassed to admit I didn't recognize him."

"Qing-Shen is a master of disguise. We shouldn't feel bad." Taji grins. "I didn't see a thing."

"I would like to see what you heard," Yoshi says.

Taji frowns, trying to remember. "He tried to disguise it, but I heard he walked with a slight limp."

"I saw he held his sword too lightly on the upswing," offers Mikko.

"I noticed he was easily distracted by girls," Kyoko adds.

I laugh.

Mei glares in my direction. "He kept looking at Kyoko and me," she says.

"I noticed it, too. Sometimes I have the same problem myself," admits Mikko, red-faced. "Though not with Mei and Kyoko."

In my heart, the White Crane screeches much louder than before. We need to hurry.

CHAPTER TEN

名誉

WHITE TIGER TEMPLE

The temple must be close now. Even though I can't hear Sensei in my head, I know he's nearby. I feel it in my bones.

"Sensei is here," I say.

"How do you know?" asks Mikko.

I can't explain it to my friends. They don't feel Sensei's touch the way I do. But they hear the confidence in my voice and know I'm not worried anymore.

Still, Kyoko worries. She asks me over and over, "Are you sure Sensei will be at the temple?"

"I'm sure," I say.

"Promise?" she asks.

But I can't do that, and nothing short of a promise will comfort Kyoko.

Beneath our feet, the path compacts into rocks: some stacked and carefully placed, all of them damp and slippery. Cautiously, I place my crutch between the stones.

Mikko notices and slips his shoulder under mine. It's much easier with someone to lean on, and Mikko has always been there for me.

The rock trail dips along the center, where many pilgrims and would-be students have walked before us.

"Do you think Sensei will be waiting on the temple steps?" Kyoko asks.

"No." Yoshi laughs. "He'll be sleeping there."

"He'll point his finger and say, 'What took you so long?'" Mikko mimics Sensei's voice perfectly.

Unexpectedly, the White Tiger Temple rears before us, gold and blue banners flapping in the wind. But there is another mountain to climb before we reach the entrance. A set of steeply sloping stairs leads to the big rain-streaked white building whose roof curves upward in a welcoming smile.

I feel at home here already.

I've been to only one other temple. We visit the Temple of the Priests of Emptiness and Nothingness when we take part in the annual Samurai Trainee Games. The Komusu priests wear baskets on their heads to show that they are separate from worldly things. They were once samurai, but have now chosen a life of peace.

We've never seen a Komusu priest with a weapon in his hand, but the whispers curl like mist around the mountains. Some people say the priests use their flutes as weapons, that the pointed end is sharp enough to stab a man through the heart. It could be true. I know Kyoko wouldn't hesitate to wield her *shakuhachi* like a dagger if we were in danger.

As I climb the final step, I see through to the courtyard beyond, where men and boys dressed in orange robes are practicing their stances. Shaolin monks openly train to fight.

The man waiting on the temple steps is wearing a long saffron-colored robe with a red sash around his ample middle. A loop of beads hangs from his neck.

"That's Abbot Lin," Mei whispers.

The abbot's clean-shaven face is brown and wrinkled, in the way skin creases and folds when it has spent too much time in the water. Time has flooded through this man's face, and his eyes shine with the same ageless wisdom we see in our teacher.

When the abbot smiles, our world fills with light. There is no darkness here.

"Greetings to you, Ki-Yaga's students. I am pleased to see you again, Mei." He gently inclines his head toward her.

Kyoko bursts into tears.

"What is wrong, child?" Abbot Lin asks.

"Sensei is really gone," she wails. "I thought he would be waiting to meet us. But he is not here."

"No, no." The abbot takes her hand. "Your master is nearby, asleep in my garden."

Yoshi grins and shrugs. *Told you so,* his shoulders say.

But I am angry. Doesn't Sensei know how worried we have been? He could at least have met us on the steps.

Inside my head Sensei laughs. *I have missed our conversations, Niya. No one else calls me to account as you do.*

Just then, Sensei emerges from the temple doorway, yawning and stretching his long spindly arms. Kyoko launches herself at him. He reels backward and barely has time to catch her.

Serves you right, I think. Sensei grins at me. He's not arguing about that. "We all get what we deserve," he says as I return his staff.

"I see you have kept your promise, Ki-Yaga. You have brought me students worthy of the task before them." There is a smile in Abbot Lin's eyes, but I can't read it. Is he making fun of us?

Sensei bows very low, full of respect. The abbot walks

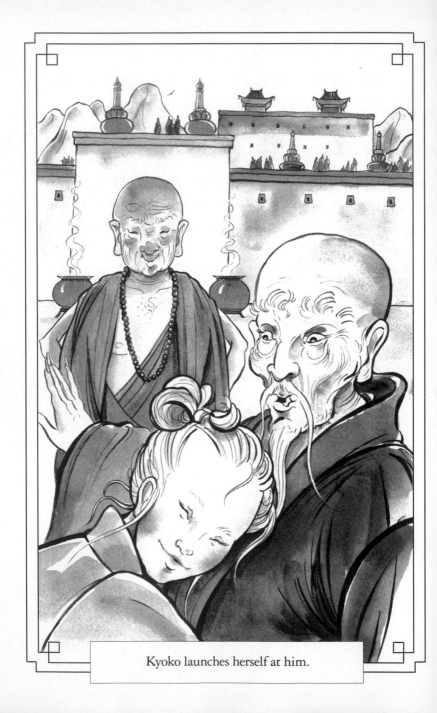

Kyoko launches herself at him.

in a slow circle around us, inspecting, muttering softly to himself.

"Yes," he finally says. "Your pupils will do very well here. A Crane, a Bat, a Snow Monkey, a Striped Gecko, and a Tiger. Shaolin has a need for them all."

"You there, young monk," the abbot calls to a boy passing through the courtyard.

"Yes, Master?" The boy is tall and skinny, like a stick insect. He's probably the same age as me, but the expression on his face is many years older.

"These children and their teacher are our honored guests. Please take them to the visitors' quarters and make sure they have everything they need."

"Will they be staying long?" the boy asks.

The abbot looks thoughtful. "As long as necessary. Many travelers have answered my call, but none have been suited to my most pressing task. These are the ones we have been waiting for. Our temple is at their service."

We stand proud to be so important to the future of the temple. Perhaps we will be given a rare and valuable treasure for safekeeping.

The boy doesn't look convinced of our special status, but I can understand that. Covered in mud and dust, we don't look as if we have come to save the day. We look more like we have come to have a bath.

"This way." We follow across the courtyard, through a garden to our sleeping quarters.

Good. As soon as we are settled, we can tell Sensei about Qing-Shen.

I know, he whispers.

Of course he does. He knows almost everything. I smile. I have missed our conversations, too.

I am watching out for him, he promises. *I will know when he is here.*

But he can't know that for certain. Qing-Shen is a great deceiver. He has already misled Sensei once and had no trouble tricking us along the road.

"Hurray!" Mikko throws himself onto the soft mattress. "I could stay here all afternoon."

Laughing, I land with a gentle thump beside him. We push and shove, try to roll each other to the floor.

"You have not come to play." Our guide looks displeased. "Abbot Lin has selected you for an important task. You should show more respect."

Kyoko and Mei exchange smiling glances. Perhaps this boy needs to go back to bed. He obviously got out on the wrong side this morning.

"You are right," Sensei says soothingly. "My students have had a long, tiring journey, and their manners are still asleep. What is your name?" Sensei asks the boy.

"Du Feng. And thank you." Du Feng presses his hands together and nods politely. But he doesn't respect us. As he leaves, he whispers to me, "Perhaps the abbot made a mistake. Maybe you are not the ones he was waiting for."

Before I can answer, Du Feng is gone.

"Did you hear that?" I ask Sensei.

"It does not matter," Sensei says. "We have more important things to talk about. Tell me about Qing-Shen."

"We met him on the road here," Yoshi says.

Sensei sits down on his mattress. "How was he?"

"Clever and charming," Mei says.

"Quick with a sword and *bo,*" adds Mikko.

Taji snorts. "He fooled us all."

"I have only ever lost one student." Our teacher folds his bottom lip inward. "I always hoped he would find his way back to me. But not like this."

"He was very interested in your traveling staff. Does he know what it hides?"

Sensei nods. "I told Qing-Shen everything."

"Why didn't he just take it then?" Taji asks.

"Qing-Shen wants much more than the jade seal. He wants revenge, and he wants me to see him triumph."

"I wish you didn't have to fight Qing-Shen, Master," I say.

Sensei curls his beard around his finger. "A teacher cannot raise his sword to strike a student. I will have to find another way to overcome Qing-Shen."

"But what if he attacks you first?" Mikko says, alarmed.

I'm worried, too. I don't want our master to fight but he needs to be able to defend himself.

"When Qing-Shen raises his blade, I will duck." Sensei grins. "I am very fast for an old man."

But we don't smile back. This is not funny at all.

"Do not worry, Little Cockroaches. I have a plan, but it is not one I can share yet," says Sensei.

After we finish unpacking, we are ready to be given our special task. But the first task the abbot finds for us is in the kitchen. If you do not work, you do not eat. Our Shaolin training has begun.

In the kitchen we meet Brother Ang, a skinny man with an even thinner smile.

"More chopping," he calls. "More peeling. More paring. The temple has many visitors, and they all want to eat."

He wields his soup ladle like a weapon, and I hate to think what he's like with a knife in his hand. Brother Ang soon has us cutting, slicing, and dicing.

"The food here mustn't be very good," Mikko whispers to Yoshi. "That string-bean cook hasn't had a decent meal for a long time."

Yoshi doesn't find a problem with the food. For every piece of carrot he throws in the pot, one goes into his mouth.

Crack-ack. Brother Ang's staff doesn't approve of Yoshi's cooking technique.

"Food is a reward for hard work," Brother Ang says. "We all eat when we have earned it."

Behind his back, Kyoko imitates him perfectly. Her imaginary soup ladle swipes toward us, and she shakes her finger right under Brother Ang's left ear.

"Stop it," I mouth when he is not looking. "You will get us in trouble."

Mei can barely hold in her laughter, and Mikko is pinching his lip hard. Even Taji, who cannot see the joke, can feel the fun and is smiling wide.

"More work. Less chatter," Brother Ang instructs. "No eating."

Sensei says the kitchen is a good place to learn, and Yoshi has already learned to eat only when Brother Ang is not looking. As soon as the monk's back is turned, Yoshi pops a fresh bamboo slice into his mouth.

"I am working hard," he mumbles. "It is hard work avoiding Brother Ang's zealous eye."

Sensei would approve. Like a good ninja, Yoshi is practicing stealth.

From behind growing stacks of sliced vegetables, I peer out to see Abbot Lin approaching. With him is a monk, arms laden with yellow-orange robes. It's a rescue mission, although not a very fashionable one.

"Put them on," the abbot says, handing us each a garment. "Then you can join the group practice in the field."

Glad to escape the kitchen, we dress quickly, pulling the robes over our jackets and baggy pants. Samurai kids dress in layers and one more layer makes little difference.

Nodding, Abbot Lin is pleased with what he sees. "All students should look the same. It is important that no one stands out. A devout monk does not attract attention to himself."

I like that. All my life I've wanted to blend in with the crowd. But it's hard to run with the same rhythm as everyone else when you've got only one leg. The robe won't make Kyoko blend in, either. Her white hair pools like honey rice around the peach-orange folds. She's by far the prettiest monk in the whole temple.

But if everyone looks the same, how can we possibly recognize Qing-Shen? Perhaps we will be gone before he tries to enter the temple. That would be good. We won't make the same mistake next time we meet a stranger on the road. In the fields, the monks are practicing in long, orderly rows. Arms and legs flying. Lunging and kicking. Punching hard at the air. There is no sense of foreboding here. Only calm. The temple is like a giant bowl of rice, simmering slowly. It waits patiently for what will be. This is a Buddhist bowl. Nothing is done in haste, and each orange grain is the same as its brother.

"Last monk on the fourth row," the abbot calls.

The monk detaches himself from the group and hurries over. It is Du Feng.

"You will teach my new students the basic movements of Shaolin," the abbot instructs.

"Yes, Master," murmurs Du Feng.

Leading us to the back of the formation, he doesn't speak. Silence is praised here at the temple, so we don't harass him with questions and even Kyoko doesn't chatter. Watching his moves closely, we copy as best we can while a monk at the front calls instructions.

It's not easy on one foot. Yoshi has no trouble as the Tiger leaps gracefully, landing on two soft paws. Nothing broken at all. Here at the White Tiger Temple, the pot is finally mended. Kick, punch. Push. Pull. Spin and turn. Begin again. Over and over we practice until my foot aches and my arms hurt.

The drill is monotonous, and nothing we do is good enough for our tutor. He's speaking to us now, but all he says is, "No, no. You must do it like this," and "You are not trying hard enough." And just for me, "Don't bother trying this. You can't kick with one leg."

"One more insult and I'm going to show him how

a samurai kid defends his honor," Mikko says through clenched teeth. "Do you want to help me, Niya?"

I grin, but inside the White Crane is not happy. I wish I had two legs. Then I'd be able to teach Du Feng a lesson.

Boom. Boom-boom.

Somewhere a gong sounds our rescue, calling us to supper. "More practice is needed. Much more practice. Meals are served in the main hall." The boy strides off. "Not that you've earned it," he calls over his shoulder.

"I'd like to practice on him," Kyoko mutters.

Even Yoshi growls softly in the direction of our tutor. Still, I bet Sensei would agree with all this practicing.

We find our master in the dining room. Sensei is thin, with limbs like a praying mantis's, but he can eat as much as Yoshi.

"Did you enjoy your afternoon lesson?" he asks, wiping a stray bean sprout from his beard.

"Our teacher does not like us," says Taji.

Sensei picks a peanut sliver from his teeth. "Sometimes the student must do the teaching."

"I don't think he wants to listen," Kyoko says grumpily.

"Who ever wanted to listen to their teacher?" Our master sighs. Pausing mid-mouthful, he places his chopsticks across his bowl. "I have the same problem all the time. Look." Sensei points to where our tutor sits eating alone. "Perhaps your teaching could begin."

"Niya should do it," suggests Yoshi.

"Yes," agrees Mikko. "He's always lecturing us."

One day I'd like to be a teacher, so I'm glad to try. Perhaps the boy would like some company.

Mei slaps me on the back. "Good luck."

I'm going to need it.

"Hello," I say, putting my bowl down on the table. "The food here is wonderful."

He looks up with a snarl. I'm not welcome.

His meal only half-finished, he rises to leave. "I do not have time to sit talking. I have work to do. I am a Shaolin monk, not a samurai kid play-acting at something he is not."

"The abbot needs us. We were asked to come here," I protest.

"Not by me. I don't need you at all. It is a waste of my time teaching you moves you cannot possibly get right with only one leg. Moves you will forget anyway once you have left the temple. I wish you'd go today," he snaps, leaving me sitting alone.

"I'm a terrible teacher," I admit, rejoining my friends.

"It is a very hard lesson," Sensei says. "You did well. You opened the book for your student."

Mikko laughs. "And he slammed it in Niya's face."

"Ah . . ." Sensei pulls at his beard. "But does anyone see the book? I believe the student has taken it with him."

You are truly an excellent teacher, Sensei whispers inside my head.

After supper we sit in meditation, each choosing the place where we feel most comfortable. Kyoko has disappeared into the forest to climb a tree and lie curled around a branch. Yoshi and Mei are sitting together on a flat rock at the back of the kitchen. Mikko has located the perfect evening gecko spot, sheltered under a bush. Taji has gone to find the Zen garden.

Zen meditation is about NOTHING. You close your eyes and empty your mind. When NOTHING is left, you are in the right place. But I can't find anywhere to bring me peace. Frustrated, I flop in the middle of the temple courtyard.

My mind is stuffed full of questions. Why do I have to be different? How can I help Sensei? And most important of all, where is Qing-Shen?

"Do you have something you wish to ask me?" The abbot settles cross-legged beside me.

I hesitate. I have so many questions.

"There is nothing you cannot ask, although there may be some questions I will not answer," the abbot says.

"Why can't I have two legs like everyone else?" I blurt.

"Because you are not like everyone else," he replies. "And the White Crane needs only one leg. You should know that."

I do. I just don't like it.

The abbot presses his hands together. Head bowed, I wait for his words.

"In Shaolin there is a saying that when you lose the right arm, the left becomes stronger. If you lose both legs, your arms become faster. If you lose both your arms and legs, your mind becomes all you need because your focus is on sharing this great wisdom with others."

He claps his hands, and I find myself looking deep into his eyes. "You can do anything you want," he says, speaking into the heart of the White Crane. "Do not waste your time counting legs. Do something that matters to you."

"I want to help Sensei. Why does Qing-Shen hate him so much?"

"It is a difficult question. Qing-Shen believes your master insulted his honor. Ki-Yaga promised to reward his pupil with the gift of his Imperial Examinations Seal. But in the end he withheld it. Many men would kill another over such an affront, let alone for such a treasure."

I shake my head. "There is more. I can feel it. Sensei's pain is much deeper than that."

"Hmm." Surprised, the abbot looks at me with his own question in his eyes. "How old is your master?" he asks.

I shrug. I don't know. Sensei is very old. "Maybe one hundred," I guess.

"Maybe more." The abbot shrugs. "I don't know, either. But in China there are some men who spend all their life trying to find the secret to immortality, and one of them is Qing-Shen. When Ki-Yaga promised to tell Qing-Shen his greatest secret, Qing-Shen thought immortality was in his grasp. Now he seeks retribution."

"So if Sensei will not tell him the secret of long life, he will end Sensei's life." I can see the balance there. If the pupil cannot be immortal, the master must die. "But Sensei is not immortal," I say. I'm sure of that. "I see him getting older every day. Sensei's secret is something else."

I don't know what it is, but it's frail and fleeting like the shadow of the *tengu*.

The abbot nods thoughtfully. "Their falling out was a great loss. Qing-Shen showed enormous skill. He could have been a master samurai swordsman. Some say as good as the famed Mitsuka Manuyoto. But Qing-Shen threw his sword away."

Qing-Shen is nothing like my friend Mitsuka. No true samurai would ever throw his sword away. It is his heart and soul. Qing-Shen's heart is not in the right place to be a samurai.

"I do not know Ki-Yaga's secret." The abbot closes his eyes. "No one does. But your master could not keep his promise when he saw the blackness inside Qing-Shen."

"Sensei has a darkness in his heart," I whisper.

Eyes snap open. "Does your master mistreat you?" the abbot asks.

"Oh, no. Nothing like that. The darkness is very deep, and it makes him sad. I'm sure it is part of the secret."

The abbot reaches out to touch my shoulder.

"Now I will answer your last question. I do not know how you can help Ki-Yaga, but I do know that one day you will."

CHAPTER ELEVEN

忠誠

SHAOLIN
SAMURAI

"Practice, practice! It's all we do around here," complains the monk sitting beside me at breakfast. "Even the sun is still in bed."

We smile in sympathy.

"It's the same at the *ryu* where we train," Mikko says, rolling his eyes.

His words make me wishful for familiar things. Honey rice pudding, the sound of the pitta birds and the smell of Sensei's noodle pancakes for breakfast. As soon as the abbot gives us our task, we'll be going home.

There's one person here I know I won't miss.

"Do you know him?" I ask, pointing to our tutor, already hard at work on his stretching exercises.

"Everyone does. That's Du Feng. He enjoys practicing." The monk smiles, adjusting his black belt. "I wish I was more like him. He's one of our most dedicated monks."

"He hopes to be assigned to teach here one day," says another. "It is a great honor that few achieve."

Groan. Double-groan. Soon Du Feng will be practicing his teaching skills on us again.

Sensei appears, waving his staff like a wand. But there is no magic in his words, only the promise of more hard work. "The abbot has prepared a busy schedule for today."

Kyoko and Mikko protest loudly.

"Busy is good." Sensei raps his staff against the wooden floor. "I do not want my students sitting around doing nothing."

"But NOTHING is good, too, Master," I say, tongue-in-cheek.

Sensei is a Zen Master. NOTHING is very important in the study of Zen. When your mind is empty, it contains all you need to know.

"How many hours did you practice when you were walking on your own?" Sensei asks.

Yoshi clenches his teeth in a guilty grin. "None."

"Then you have already spent many days doing NOTHING. Chop, chop, Little Cockroaches."

It's hard to argue with Sensei. He's a master of swordsmanship, but sometimes I think he's even more dangerous with words.

"Another day with Du Feng." I sigh.

"You two have a lot in common," says Sensei.

"We do not," I object. "He's rude and obnoxious."

"And grumpy and cantankerous," adds Mei.

Sensei raps his staff on the wooden floor again. Twice as hard. "If you don't like what you see, you should look differently. Imagine Du Feng is a chicken."

"*Cluck-cluck. Cluck-cluck.*" Kyoko makes us all laugh.

"But Du Feng is not a chicken," points out Yoshi.

"If one boy can be a Tiger, then another can be a chicken. What happens if you place a chicken in your lap and stroke its head?"

"I know. My family has many chickens, and it is my job to look after them," says Mei. "It will sit there quietly."

"So why," Sensei asks, "would a chicken bite and peck instead of sitting?"

"If it was in pain," suggests Kyoko.

Understanding strikes louder than the breakfast gong. This morning, no matter how nasty he is to me, I will try to find out why Du Feng is hurting.

"You cannot count your chicken before it hatches," Sensei says. "But eventually the shell breaks open. And when it does, you should be there to help it."

Boom-boom. The call to early-morning exercise echoes through the temple.

Out on the practice field, we're in the back row so Du Feng can whisper explanations without interrupting his fellow monks.

"Horse stance," the instructor bellows.

Du Feng spreads his legs, knees to the side, and crouches low. "As if you're riding a horse."

That's easy. We've already been practicing this one most of the way here. We bend deep, arms out in front. *In, out. In, out.* Our arms retract and extend with our breathing. Slowly, our instructor counts to ten.

"Breathing is very important," our tutor says.

"We know." Kyoko giggles. "That's why we do it every day. Lots and lots of practice breaths."

Du Feng glares, but Kyoko parries with a smile. A smile from a samurai girl is much harder to dodge than the swipe of a sword. A Shaolin boy is a sitting duck. Even if he is a chicken.

"Bow and Arrow. Crouching Cat." On and on, the instructor calls the stances. "Three Pillars. Seven Stars." There's lots of counting. We bend our legs and count. We stretch back and count. And we count the minutes until it's over.

"One-Thousand-Day Stretch," the instructor shouts.

"Breathing is very important," our tutor says.

Taji raises an eyebrow. We can't possibly count that high. We'd be here until nightfall.

"The abbot says that if you do this exercise for a thousand days, then you will be able to touch your toes with your forehead," Du Feng snaps. "You must pay better attention. It is important to be flexible. No wonder a samurai kid cannot leap and lunge like a Shaolin warrior."

He looks at my one leg, saying nothing. But the White Crane hears the contempt anyway.

It doesn't matter because we don't need his help. We have each other.

"Left leg out straight," Mikko whispers to help Taji.

I'm the one who needs the most assistance. I haven't got a left leg.

"Bend down on your right leg."

I can do that.

"Change legs."

This is definitely not the exercise for me.

Yoshi doesn't like it, either. "I'm not doing this for a thousand days," he insists.

"A thousand days is not very long," teases Mei. "It's less than three years."

When you're doing this exercise, even three minutes is forever.

"No talking," Du Feng hisses. "Your form work is so poor that you have no time to spend discussing it."

Still, this is the perfect place for Yoshi. The White Tiger Temple monks don't fight to hurt anyone. Their moves are all about defense.

"Would a monk ever fight to kill?" he asks.

"Not unless it was absolutely necessary," Du Feng says. "Buddha taught us to exercise for fitness and health. But when the time comes to defend the temple, we will not hesitate."

I've seen Shaolin warriors practicing with swords in their mouths and knives between their toes, but they prefer not to use standard weapons. They like to use ordinary things—a spade, a rake, or even a frying pan. We thought Sensei was clever when he showed Mikko how to make a funeral gong out of a cooking pot, but here, what holds rice one day is a lethal weapon the next.

For our first lesson in fighting forms, we place our swords on the ground. We turn in slow circles, practicing the new movements. We learn to redirect an attacker's blow. To make claw hands and iron fists. We learn to push an opponent aside when he is off-balance.

Softly, softly. It's nothing like the jarring clash of swords.

"If this is the best you can do, you should give up," Du Feng says grumpily.

By midday we are stiff and sore. And starving. Lunch is a meal of steamed vegetables and rice, cooked in a deadly weapon. Looking around the meal room, Sensei is nowhere to be seen, and Du Feng is sitting by himself again. Others might admire him, but no one seeks his company.

"Let's sit with Du Feng," Mei suggests.

"Do you mind if we sit here?" Yoshi asks, placing his piled plate on the table beside our tutor.

The boy grunts into his bowl. Yes, he does mind. But we ignore that and surround him so he can't escape.

"Do you know Qing-Shen?" Mei asks. "I've heard he was a student here once. Many years ago, before I came."

Du Feng spits on the ground. He likes Qing-Shen even less than we do. "Qing-Shen sneaks like a toad. He wriggles like a worm. . . ."

"No leaping like a panther?" asks Mikko, grinning.

"Or flying like an eagle?" suggests Kyoko, arms out like wings.

"We heard he is faster than the wind. That he comes and goes with the night breeze," Taji says.

Du Feng snorts. "The only air around Qing-Shen is the hot air he blows himself."

"He is not a man of honor," Yoshi agrees.

Turning angrily to Yoshi, Du Feng is not interested in our opinion. "What would a samurai know of such things? A samurai hides behind his sword, but a Shaolin monk is brave with his bare hands. Anyone can learn to use a weapon. It is much harder to lay the weapon aside."

We already know that because Sensei taught us.

"A true samurai doesn't need a sword," Yoshi whispers. But he doesn't pick a fight here and now. That's not the way Yoshi does things. He'll find another way to show Du Feng what honor means to a samurai.

After lunch we are sent to work in the vegetable garden. Four young monks are already there, and I'm relieved to see Du Feng is not among them. The monks are gathering cabbage, mustard greens, and radishes. It's comfortable, familiar work. The early afternoon sun traces warm patterns on my back, and our companions are friendly and talkative.

"How does it feel to be a Shaolin monk?" the tallest boy asks. "Was it worth the long journey?"

"Yes," says Mikko. "Even though every muscle I have aches, I have learned many useful new skills."

Plonk. A cabbage lands in the bamboo basket. "The work is hard, but the rewards are great," the youngest monk says. "We are fortunate to live in such a family. At home I have no brothers and sisters, but here I have more than fifty."

"You were a student here once before, weren't you?" the tall boy asks Mei. "Do you remember your first sparring partner?"

"I've never forgotten," she says. "You whacked me in the face with your fist."

The monk looks apologetic. "I was clumsy and inexperienced. It was an accident."

"I know," she says. "You would not be still standing if I didn't think so."

Plonk-plonk. The basket is almost full.

Another monk looks up from the row of carrots. "There are many people passing through the temple this month. The abbot says a great danger is coming and he must distribute our treasure for safekeeping. You are the only visitors to stay and train with us."

"We are just waiting to see what we will be given. Then we will be on our way, too," says Yoshi.

"Except me." *Plonk.* Mei throws the last cabbage. "I'm staying."

"Even if it's dangerous?" Yoshi's face is worried. He doesn't want her to stay.

"I have to, Yoshi. I belong here. You know how it feels when you find where you belong?"

Yoshi shakes his head. He hasn't found that place yet.

But I have and I understand. I belong at the Cockroach Ryu. If Sensei will let me, I'll stay there forever.

"You are lucky to have Du Feng as a tutor." The tall monk tugs at a radish. "He can break a rock with his bare hands."

It's hard to believe anyone can do that, but I've heard it said of the most skilled monks.

Yoshi looks impressed, and even Mikko is paying close attention.

"I have sat in many of his lessons," says the youngest monk. "He is a patient and kind teacher."

That's even harder to believe.

"But no one seems to like him. He never has any friends to sit or walk with," says Taji.

The monk looks horrified. "Oh, no. We would not want to interrupt the thoughts of one so devout."

"We are not worthy to speak with Du Feng." The youngest monk is wishful, admiring.

"Everyone needs friends," I say. "If Shaolin is a family, who is being a brother to Du Feng? Maybe he is lonely."

The monks look at me with surprise. "I never considered that," the nearest one says.

I am a good teacher after all.

I know, Sensei whispers inside my head. *I taught you.*

Looking up, I see Du Feng hurrying toward us. "Abbot Lin requests your presence in the Garden of Five Lights," he announces, turning before we have a chance to respond.

"Where is it?" Yoshi calls.

"You're a clever samurai warrior. Find it yourself," Du Feng retorts.

"Did you hear that?" Mikko asks the monks.

"Yes." The tall monk watches Du Feng walking away. "He is teaching you resourcefulness."

Hmph. Mikko snorts, and I agree with him. Perhaps we will be resourceful enough to find a way to teach Du Feng a lesson.

"This afternoon, you will study animal forms," the abbot says. "There is much to be learned by watching and imitating the movements of animals. You will learn to be the snake, the leopard, the tiger . . ."

Beside me Yoshi growls, pleased. He likes the sound of that.

". . . the crane . . ."

I stand taller than before. My spirit soars across Song Shan.

". . . and the dragon."

I plummet back to earth. No way. No Cockroach will ever be a dragon.

The abbot hasn't finished talking. "Then you will learn many more movements. You will learn the one hundred seventy-two combinations of empty hands and the eighteen arms of *wushu*. . . ."

Here in the White Tiger Temple, the counting never ends.

"And perhaps"—the abbot smiles at Kyoko—"you will learn to make the dreaded Monkey Fist."

Mikko grins at me. Kyoko already knows that one. We both have bruises on our arm to prove it.

"Each of you must choose an animal form to study," Sensei instructs us.

My decision is already made. I am the crane.

Yoshi chooses the tiger, of course. And Mei follows him. Always at home in the trees, Kyoko chooses the panther. Mikko selects the snake. It's a good choice. The snake is a lizard without arms or legs, and Mikko is the Striped Gecko, with one arm missing.

Only Taji is thoughtful. "I will be the dragon," he finally says.

"W-what?" I splutter. "You can't be a dragon. It's dishonorable."

"Your head is still full of noodles." Taji laughs. "Remember when you said the same thing about ninja? Have you forgotten your own lesson? You must look differently if you want to see what is good. Maybe one day I will replace the Dragon Master."

Sensei nods. "Excellent. Together you will know all of the animal forms."

The abbot nods, too. "If the heart of the dragon is pure, then its fire will be all the colors of the rainbow."

He claps his hands, and our instructors for the afternoon come running. *Oh, no.* My teacher is Du Feng. Reluctantly, I follow him into the temple courtyard. I've had enough of his insults.

"If you're going to be rude, I'm not staying," I say. "I'd rather be a dragon."

"I didn't choose to spend the afternoon with you, either," Du Feng says. "But I have to do as my abbot instructs. So let's get this done as quickly as possible."

I nod. For once we're in agreement.

"One day a monk was working when a crane landed nearby," Du Feng begins. "He tried to frighten the crane away."

Why would he do that? The White Crane within me listens intently.

"The monk used sticks. He tried to hit the crane on the head, but it dodged, blocking with its wings. He tried to hit the crane's wings, but it stepped aside and obstructed with its talons. The monk tried to poke at the crane's body, but the clever bird stepped back and bit at the stick with its beak."

Du Feng stops to check that I am listening.

"Please continue," I say, eager to hear more.

"From then on, the monk studied the crane to learn new techniques of defense."

Inside me, the White Crane tucks its head under its fighting wing and returns to sleep. It has learned nothing it did not know already. But I am learning a great deal as Du Feng demonstrates the crane movements. I do my best to copy.

"You have a smattering of talent," Du Feng admits. "But it takes at least a decade of training to learn the white crane form, and I doubt a samurai kid could concentrate for that long."

Nothing I do will ever be good enough for Du Feng. "Why don't you like us?" I demand.

He studies my face but says nothing. His eyes are dark like Mei's, but they don't twinkle. They glimmer with concentration, the way a sparrow watches for the hawk's first move.

"I want to know," I insist.

"All right. I'll tell you. I have been here studying hard for five years. Five years of hard work and no master has ever noticed me. I am given the most difficult tasks but not a word of encouragement. Then you and your friends swagger in, and immediately you become the center of attention. It's not fair."

Du Feng's face is sad. I feel sorry for him. If I was treated like that, I'd be jealous, too.

"I am always overlooked," he whispers. "The abbot does not even remember my name."

"I thought that not to be noticed was the way of the Shaolin monk," I say. "I wish I could fade into the background."

Du Feng sighs. "It is true one should not strive to draw attention. But just sometimes, I would like to know that I am doing well."

"Your abbot is a wise man who knows many things. I'm sure he knows your name. And your brother monks admire you a lot."

Du Feng doesn't look convinced.

"You don't really want to be noticed like me," I say. "It's not easy to have one leg. Close your eyes."

He closes his lids.

"Now stand on one leg."

I am the teacher now. Cautiously, Du Feng does as I say.

"Raise your leg higher. Imagine a Shaolin flying leap."

I know he can see me in his mind, flat on my face in the dirt. But Du Feng doesn't laugh.

"It is not the same thing. You're not like me at all," he says, striding off. Halfway across the courtyard, he stops, looking back. "You'll never be a Shaolin warrior," he calls.

"Kids with one leg don't swagger," I yell. "We hop."

In another corner of the courtyard, Sensei has been teaching origami to a group of monks. My friends are already there. Only Mei is missing. She is practicing with the advanced classes in the Hall of One Hundred Fists.

"How did your lesson go?" Sensei asks as I flop beside him.

"I learned much about the White Crane," I say.

"And what did your student learn?"

"Nothing," I admit. "I am not a good teacher after all."

Sensei finishes folding a crane and passes it to me.

"The lesson is not over yet. When you have made one thousand cranes, then you will find peace and happiness."

"And what about when you have made one thousand lizards?" asks Mikko.

"Then you will have sore fingers," I say, grinning.

"One crane was always enough trouble for me, anyway." Mikko pokes me in the ribs. "My arms are so sore, I don't think I could even draw my sword."

"My feet ache from kicking," moans Taji.

"My hands hurt from punching," I mutter.

Yoshi just groans.

Kyoko sighs. "My ankles ache from dodging and weaving."

For once Sensei doesn't lecture us to stop complaining. He smiles. "Now you are truly Shaolin samurai."

But not if Du Feng has any say about it.

CHAPTER TWELVE

義

BUDDHA'S CAVE

The gong calls the monks to morning meditation and exercise long before the sun has had a chance to rub its eyes and get out of bed. *Boom-oom-oom.* Bleary-eyed, I stumble to my crutch.

"What's the emergency?" Mikko rolls from his mat, hand on his sword and ready for battle.

Not Yoshi. He's still snoring away.

Mei, Kyoko, and Taji are awake, too. It's a good thing, as it will take all five of us to tip Yoshi from his bed.

He lands with a thump and wakes with a yell.

"Hurry up," we chorus. "Du Feng will be even more bad-tempered if we are late."

"Breakfast?" Yoshi asks hopefully.

"More practice!" we chorus.

The field is already furrowed with rows of orange. Du Feng is waiting, frowning, arms crossed. An instructor calls orders, and we begin stretching exercises. Counting the moves and every minute until breakfast.

"You will never get this right." Du Feng fixes Kyoko's stance and prods Yoshi's fist into place. He's pretty brave to do that, especially when Yoshi is still half asleep and hasn't had anything to eat yet.

"What about this?" Mei asks. "Is my arm high enough?"

Du Feng grunts. There's nothing wrong with Mei's morning form work, but he would never admit it.

Taji makes a face when Du Feng is not looking. "Our tutor got out of bed on the wrong side again this morning."

Every morning, if you ask me.

"Lucky him," Yoshi growls. "I didn't get any choice."

Finally, it's time for breakfast: buckwheat porridge latticed with slices of peach and pear. The monks don't eat meat, and they don't use flavoring or spices. There's plenty of fruit and vegetables but no sushi or honey-rice pudding here.

"I'm in pain already, and the day has barely begun." Mikko rubs the backs of his knees.

"Then you will be pleased to know you will spend the next hour sitting in the temple study hall. Painting, poetry, and calligraphy are the three perfections of the Middle Kingdom," says Sensei.

Mikko and I groan. Poetry is the worst exercise of all. It stretches your brain until it hurts.

"Practice makes perfect." Sensei claps his hands.

There's nothing perfect about my handwriting, no matter how hard I try. My page is soon a splatter of grimy splotches. Even with one hand, Mikko does much better than me.

"Your brushwork looks like crane droppings," Sensei says.

I grin. I have learned to look at things differently. To find something good in everything.

"Thank you, Sensei. I am rewarded by your words. It is not easy to draw crane droppings in ink."

Smiling, Sensei moves on to check Yoshi's work.

"Good morning, young samurai students." Abbot Lin's voice booms though the doorway, closely followed by the abbot himself. "I have something special planned for this morning. You will journey up the mountain to the cave where Buddha sat meditating for nine years. Many people have found answers to problems there. Unfortunately, I have to cancel your poetry lesson, as you will need to leave immediately." The abbot winks at me. "I hope you are not too disappointed."

It's impossible to hide our excitement. We would much rather walk in the sun than sit inside sorting words.

"Young monk," the abbot calls to our tutor, practicing nearby. "You will accompany the new students to Buddha's cave."

"Yes, Master." Du Feng bows obediently, but he is not pleased. "You don't deserve to enter Buddha's cave," he whispers after Abbot Lin has left. "Others have to work hard to earn the privilege. I have never been asked to go, but everything is given to you."

Taji shakes his finger, teasing. "You must learn to listen, Du Feng. You *have* been invited to the cave. I heard the abbot ask you just then."

Du Feng scowls, but his look of displeasure is wasted on Taji, who can't see it anyway.

"Are you coming, Sensei?" I ask, hopeful. Perhaps our teacher will walk between us and Du Feng's bad temper.

Sensei shakes his head. "I have been to the cave many times. My answers are not waiting there." Sadness slips across his eyes, and Sensei blinks quickly to hide it. The shadow is gone, but the White Crane knows what it saw.

Du Feng strides ahead, walking so quickly that we struggle to keep up. The path slithers and snakes through the forest grove. A sense of peacefulness drops from the trees onto our shoulders.

"Where are we?" Kyoko breathes deep. Even the air tastes better here.

On both sides of the path, great stone monuments watch in silence.

"These are the burial *stupa* of past abbots and some of the temple's most esteemed monks," Du Feng says. "You would not understand."

He's wrong. Some things don't need to be understood. You can feel them.

"Keep moving," orders Du Feng. "I do not have all day to spend here. Unlike some others, I have work to do."

"We've been working," Yoshi argues. "My arms ache from lugging sacks of rice for Brother Ang."

"And I've scrubbed more pots and pans than I knew existed," complains Kyoko.

But Du Feng doesn't listen to our protests, clambering up the rocks ahead.

No one offers me a hand, but Taji gives me a shove

from behind and Yoshi laughs as I scramble to find my footing.

We ignore Du Feng. There is no point in including him in our conversation. He never has anything helpful to say.

"Do you think the abbot will give us our task this afternoon?" Kyoko asks.

"I hope so," says Taji. "Then we can leave before Qing-Shen arrives."

Mei sighs. "But that won't make him give up. He'll follow wherever you go."

"True," agrees Yoshi. "But out on the road, we will be more likely to recognize him. He will not have the same element of surprise."

There's no way we would let him fool us twice.

"Perhaps the abbot does not need you anymore," Du Feng calls back. "Maybe he saw you practicing and decided you are not worthy."

"I'm trying to like him." Kyoko clenches her fists.

"Some things are harder than others," I say.

"No." Mikko laughs. "Some things are impossible."

Up ahead, Du Feng says nothing. But we know he heard.

"Almost there," he finally calls. "If you stop chattering, you will climb much quicker."

Yoshi smiles at me. We're not in a hurry.

The entrance to Buddha's Cave is small, one person wide, but inside, we all fit easily, with room to spare.

"There's nothing here," says Kyoko, disappointed. "It's empty."

Du Feng sits cross-legged, facing the far wall.

"What do *we* do?" Mikko asks impatiently.

Mei puts her fingers to her lips. "Du Feng is meditating. We need to be quiet."

"Let's go exploring," suggests Kyoko. "Du Feng will find us when he is ready."

I agree with Kyoko and, this time, even Mikko doesn't argue with her.

"Are you coming, Mei?" I ask.

She nods.

"Me too," adds Taji.

Yoshi is already waiting at the cave entrance.

Setting a fast pace, Kyoko leads the way farther up the mountain path. Sun weaves its fingers through the leaves to tap us on the shoulder. But there is nothing fragile about this peace and quiet. It's as solid as the great rock walls towering above the trees. It would take an enormous blow to make even a little crack.

Suddenly, Taji stops. Concentrating. Listening hard.

"What's wrong?" Mikko asks.

"Something is coming down the mountain. Something big. The path is vibrating," says Taji.

And now we can all hear it. A low rumble. Growing, until even the mountain is trembling in fear. Stones rattle down the ridge, racing away from whatever chases them. My foot wants to run, too.

"Quick. Get off the path," Taji bellows. "Now."

Panicking, Mei turns, disoriented.

"Not that way." Yoshi reaches out to grab her as we all scramble into the undergrowth.

Closer, closer. The ground shakes as danger roars toward us.

"What is it?" Mei's eyes are bright with fear.

Taji shakes his head.

We huddle together, hoping we're safe here.

"I'm afraid," admits Mikko.

"Me too," I say. The White Crane rolls into a tight ball, hiding its face under a wing. "We're all afraid."

A massive boulder hurtles past, barely two slipper

lengths from where we crouch. It misses the bend and careens off down the hillside, sending rock and rubble spinning after it.

For a moment, we are too shocked to move. Then Kyoko starts to shiver. Putting my arm around her shoulders, I hold her tight and still.

"It would have taken us with it," she whispers.

It's quiet again, but this time it's an uneasy peace as we strain to listen for another warning sound.

"Not yet," Taji says when Yoshi rises.

It seems like forever before Taji says, "It's safe."

Cautiously, I step back onto the path.

"We were so lucky." Yoshi looks over the cliff edge. "That boulder flattened everything in front of it. It would have flattened us, too."

Blood drips from a large scratch on Mikko's leg, and Taji has cuts on his face. But no one complains. We're glad to be alive.

"What's this?" Mei pulls a familiar silk flag from a branch. "Even the mountain is delivering Qing-Shen's messages."

"Qing-Shen must have dislodged that boulder," says

Mikko. "Why is he trying to kill us? His argument is with Sensei."

I shake my head. "It's more complicated than that. Du Feng is jealous of the attention we are receiving from the abbot." I pause. "Imagine how Qing-Shen must feel when he sees us with Sensei."

"We have replaced him." Taji understands immediately, but the others are unsure.

"What do you mean?" asks Mei.

"Qing-Shen wanted Sensei's treasure and his secret knowledge, but our teacher turned him away. Now Sensei has chosen us," explains Taji.

"But he hasn't given us any treasure or secret knowledge," protests Kyoko. "We don't even want it."

"One thing is certain," I say. "Our master is in great danger."

Mei bites her lip. "And Sensei won't lift a sword against his ex-student," she reminds us.

"Then I will do it for him." Yoshi places his hand on his weapon.

"But you never fight," I say.

"Remember how everyone else has found a spirit

guide, but I have none? Then the night you almost died on our mountain, the Tiger came and showed me what to do."

We nod. I remember it as if it was yesterday.

"The Tiger has found me again. Sensei needs my help this time." Yoshi crosses his arms, a determined look on his face. "I have to fight Qing-Shen for him. It is my chance to put things right for myself *and* our teacher."

Now that we know our enemy is here on the mountain, Mikko is eager to draw his sword, too. "Qing-Shen might be farther along the track. Perhaps we can catch up with him. We can make sure he never even gets close to Sensei."

Mei looks unconvinced. "Qing-Shen is probably long gone."

"And if he's not, he'll be waiting for us. We'd be walking into a trap," I say.

Ear to the ground, Taji is not listening to our conversation. "Someone's coming."

Now China's Warrior is hunting us.

"Where are you?" Du Feng's irritated voice curls up the path. "We need to begin our climb back down."

For the first time ever, we're glad to see him.

"Didn't you hear the huge noise?" Mei asks as Du Feng appears. "Didn't you feel the ground shake?"

"I don't know why the abbot bothered to send you up here." Du Feng sighs. "You learned nothing from the cave. Of course, I didn't expect you would."

"Run!" Taji interrupts with a yell. "Another boulder is coming."

Kyoko tugs Du Feng toward the edge of the path. "Hurry." But our tutor stands and pushes her arm away, shaking his head at us as we press back into the undergrowth.

"There are never rockfalls here. Except perhaps in your head."

The path shivers. The trees tremble. Around me the world shifts and a great noise roars down the mountain. The exasperation on Du Feng's face turns to panic.

"Move!" Mei screams.

"Now!" Yoshi bellows.

But Du Feng is frozen in the wrong place. He's going to be killed if he stays there. Desperately, I throw myself into him, knocking us both off the path and toward the cliff side. Grasping at the low bushes, I slow our roll just before we reach the edge.

Desperately, I throw myself into him.

My heart claws its way up to my throat. It's scary looking down, but it's even more frightening looking back at the path. The massive boulder barrels through the space where we recently stood. Shaken, Du Feng lets Yoshi help him to his feet.

"Thanks," he mutters, turning to me. "You saved my life."

"That's all right. You would have done the same," I say.

Du Feng looks thoughtful. "No. I would not have. I am not that brave."

Mikko reaches his hand out to me, and I hop up, only to collapse down again.

"What's wrong?" Taji asks.

"I twisted my ankle."

Nothing serious but difficult when you've only got one.

"We'll have to carry you back," Yoshi decides.

"What if we make a hammock chair out of our robes?" suggests Mei.

Sometimes it's good to have two layers of clothing. Kyoko quickly ties the knots, and soon the chair is made. Yoshi takes one end, and Du Feng moves to take the other.

Head down, he looks like he's about to cry. Sometimes I forget that our tutor is just a kid, like us.

"What's wrong?" Kyoko places her hand on his. Our cheeky monkey has a heart as soft as snow, but it's warm enough to melt even Du Feng's resistance.

"I am ashamed." He looks directly at me. "I have not treated you well."

"I was angry and rude, too," I admit. "I didn't say it aloud, but I thought some very insulting things. No one is perfect."

"But a Shaolin monk should be." Du Feng looks away.

"The other monks think you are a wonderful example," Taji says.

Sniffing loudly, Du Feng shakes his bowed head.

"In fact," Mikko says with a chuckle, "we're a bit sick of hearing how terrific you are. No one is that good."

Finally, our tutor looks up. And almost smiles.

"Thank you. Again," he mumbles. "We should get Niya back to the temple. Our monks are famed healers and will soon have him on his foot again."

Yoshi whistles as he walks, and one by one, we all join in. Even Du Feng.

Water trickles down the face of the rock walls. The
world is freshly washed, clean and pure. This is a place
where new things grow twice as fast. Even friendship.

Mouth open, Sensei snores in the abbot's garden.

"How come Sensei never has to do any work?"
whispers Mikko.

"Ah, but I am teaching my students to be careful what
they say. You never know who might hear." Sensei opens
one eye. "Some of my students are very slow learners."

It's a good thing he's awake, as we need to tell him
our news.

"Qing-Shen was on the mountain," I say.

Sensei puts his finger to his lips. He has other
priorities.

"Did you find what you needed to know?" Sensei asks
Du Feng.

He bows low. "Yes, Master."

Reaching forward, Sensei takes the boy's hand in his.
"You might be surprised what the abbot knows about
you."

Shaking his head, Du Feng smiles. "It doesn't matter anymore. Now I understand that it is myself I must impress, not my abbot. I, too, am a slow learner."

Sensei grins. "In my experience a lesson learned slowly is a lesson never forgotten."

"Thank you, Sensei. I must go and complete my kitchen duties, or Brother Ang will teach me a lesson I do not want to learn. I will also arrange a salve for Niya's twisted ankle." Du Feng hurries off in the direction of the kitchen, his orange robe flapping.

"Poor Du Feng." Kyoko sighs.

"Du Feng is one of the abbot's most trusted and promising students. He who thinks he is least is more often first," says Sensei. "Now, tell me about Qing-Shen and how Niya injured himself."

"Qing-Shen sent a huge boulder hurtling down the path we were walking on." Mikko grips his sword hilt until his knuckles turn white.

"And then he dislodged another boulder, and it almost knocked Niya and Du Feng down the mountain. That's when Niya sprained his ankle," says Mei.

"Why didn't you warn us what Qing-Shen might do?" I demand.

"I did much better than that," says Sensei. "I taught you to work it out yourself."

"But in the end we achieved nothing," I say.

"Perfect." Sensei nods, satisfied with the lesson.

"How can that be good?" I ask. "Qing-Shen is here, ready to strike again."

Sensei smiles. "Yes. NOTHING will stand in his way."

NOTHING is important to a Zen master. Sometimes Zen seems too silly for words. But that's the whole point. You have to see past the words, and Yoshi's face tells me he understands.

He is ready to meet Qing-Shen.

The gong sounds again. "Niya can stay and rest his foot, but for everyone else . . . more practice." Sensei waves my friends away.

"Aren't you worried about Qing-Shen, Master?" I ask.

"No," he says. "I am not. I am glad to be a little closer to what I must do."

I wait, hoping Sensei will continue talking.

"When I first came to our mountain, I was rolling a great burden before me," he says. "I pushed it to the top and there I rested. I looked around and saw where I would teach. I built the Cockroach Ryu. But now I am on my way down the mountain, and when the time comes for me to leave the *ryu,* momentum will keep my work rolling."

"But who will take your place?" I ask. "Even Qing-Shen failed that test."

"Maybe it will be you." Sensei smiles.

I laugh, and he chuckles with me. As if my one foot could fill Sensei's shoes.

CHAPTER THIRTEEN

礼

CHINA'S WARRIOR

The abbot has given us an hour to rest. My ankle is stronger today, and I can easily hop on it. But a break from practice is welcome anytime.

It's warm lying on the grass under the afternoon sun. An ant tickles as it wipes its feet on my hand. But I can't relax. Too many unfinished sentences hang over my head. The confrontation with Qing-Shen. Leaving the temple and Du Feng. Saying good-bye to Mei. I don't like any of the endings threatening to drop down on me.

I roll over to face Mei. "I was surprised when you said you were going to stay here. I thought you would return to your village after we left."

"What would I do that for?" She seems amused. "Why wouldn't I stay?"

"Well, you know, girls usually get married and . . ." I hesitate. Kyoko is paying close attention, and wedged between Mei and her, I feel trapped.

"You mean girls wouldn't be suited to a warrior life?" Kyoko is ready to pounce.

Taji, Mikko, and Yoshi are grinning. But not me. I'm in a perilous situation. It's dangerous to offend one girl.

How much worse to offend two? Two is definitely not a lucky number now.

"No, no." I retreat as fast as I can with one leg and a big mouth. "Girls make great warriors."

"It's okay," Mei says. "No one will marry me anyway. I'm too ugly."

That's not true. She's not beautiful like Kyoko, but she's not ugly.

Mei stretches out a foot and kicks off her slipper. "See how big my feet are? Only a farmer would want a wife with feet like that. And my father is an important man. He will not let me marry anyone less than a government official."

"But your feet are nowhere near as big as Kyoko's," I say. Then I realize my mistake. Kyoko's foot kicks hard, and I am within easy range. "And Kyoko's feet are very attractive," I quickly add.

"Why would a husband care about foot size?" asks Yoshi.

"In the Middle Kingdom, small feet are a symbol of beauty. Most women bind their feet from the time they are four. Every day they rebind them tightly. Then the

girl will have feet that curl like the leaves of the lotus."
Mei uses a stick to draw a picture. "Like this."

"Ugh." Taji shudders. He doesn't need an image to
see the deformity.

"That doesn't look like a flower," says Mikko. "I think
you would have ugly feet if you did that. Your feet are
fine."

Mei smiles, and Yoshi pats Mikko on the back.

"My father remembers when none of the village
women bound their feet." Mei wriggles her toes. "He
says we are too poor to allow our women to be slaves to
such ideals. Women must be fit and strong to stand long
hours in the field. But I think it is more than that. My
father is a big man with a huge heart and he would not
like to see young girls in pain. He says he forgot to begin
the binding of my feet and now it is too late."

"Your father knows you are already beautiful enough,"
says Kyoko. "Someone will marry you one day. Niya's
sister wants to marry Mikko. That proves there's hope
for all of us."

Mikko pulls Kyoko's hair. "Ouch!"

Kyoko tugs Mikko's ear until Yoshi makes them stop.
"Yeow!"

Lying in the meadow, toes tucked into the grass, none of us wants to go home yet. But we can't stay. We came to leave. Soon Abbot Lin will give us a part of the temple for safekeeping and we'll be on our way.

If Qing-Shen lets us.

"I wonder where Qing-Shen is now," I say.

We haven't seen or heard anything since yesterday on the mountain.

"He is preparing his next move," suggests Mikko. "That's what I would be doing."

Yoshi picks a flower and hands it to Mei. "Qing-Shen is drawing closer. I can sense him coming."

"We should do as General Chu advised us," counsels Taji. "If we look through Qing-Shen's eyes, we will be able to work out where he is." Taji leans back, arms behind his head, eyes closed. "Help me find him."

One by one, we contribute what we know, building the picture inside Taji's head.

"Qing-Shen is clever and resourceful," says Mikko. "Sensei taught him the way of the sword."

"Sensei also taught him the skills of a ninja," Kyoko says.

"And Sensei taught him to listen with his eyes," I say.

"And to see with his ears," adds Yoshi.

"He has been taught everything Sensei knows," Mei whispers.

Together we don't have even half of Sensei's knowledge. But do we know enough to help Yoshi defeat Qing-Shen?

Taji sits up. "I've found him."

"Where?" Yoshi asks, his eyes bright with determination.

"Remember how at Toyozawa Castle the ninja worked in the kitchen? Sensei said it was because they knew that the best place to hide is under the nose of anyone who might be looking for you," says Taji. "Qing-Shen is already here with us."

But where?

Orange robes fill the fields, the courtyard, the kitchen—all the rooms in the temple. Everyone looks the same to us. Surely the monks would know if a stranger was in their midst. Or perhaps they would just think it was another pilgrim answering the abbot's call for help.

"What should we do, Niya?" Yoshi asks.

I think faster than I ever have before. It's as if I can feel

Qing-Shen breathing on my neck and hear his laughter mocking us.

"Qing-Shen wants to kill our master. But just as much, he wants to possess Sensei's treasure and secret. And watch Sensei suffer seeing them stolen. Qing-Shen will start with the easiest task. He knows where to find the jade seal."

The secret compartment in our teacher's traveling staff.

"But he knows Sensei's sword will always protect his staff. And a samurai is never apart from his sword. Not even when he is asleep," says Mikko.

My friends smile, feeling safe. But not for long.

I shake my head. "Sensei takes his sword off to bathe."

Six smiles fall at my feet.

"Sensei is in the bathhouse now," Kyoko whispers.

We run as fast as we can.

The man standing before Sensei is small, but everything about him glitters. He is not hiding now. He is gloating.

Qing-Shen wears an ornate jacket embroidered with gold thread. His trousers are expensive silk. Red and bronze eagles stretch from ankle to waist, their wingtips ablaze with burnished flame.

"All that glitters is not gold," I mutter, reminding my friends of the lesson Sensei taught us on the road to Toyozawa.

The glitter in Qing-Shen's eyes is midnight black. Cold and calculating like a snake, his tongue flickers across damp lips as he eyes his cornered prey.

Our teacher sits in the bath, completely naked. Not a thread in sight, not a stitch of any kind.

"I thought when this moment came, I would at least be dressed for the occasion." Kyoko hands him a towel, and Sensei rises.

"NOTHING matters, Master," I say. "A true samurai does not need a sword, nor does a real warrior wear silk pants."

Qing-Shen snarls softly.

Yoshi growls, louder. He moves to stand between Qing-Shen and Sensei.

"Out of my way," Qing-Shen snaps. "My quarrel is not with you."

"Neither is it with a man who does not even have a weapon." Yoshi doesn't move from the place he was destined to find. He stands solid as an oak tree. No amount of hot air can ruffle his leaves.

"I thought a true samurai didn't need a sword," Qing-Shen sneers.

"It is true," Yoshi agrees. "He needs only the courage of a friend. You have no friends in this room, so you will be forced to rely on your sword."

"I saw your friends' courage on the mountain yesterday. I watched as they crawled into the forest like cowardly caterpillars." He laughs.

"Even the caterpillar eventually flies," Sensei murmurs, flapping his arms and almost losing his towel.

Kyoko stifles a giggle, and Mikko struggles to keep a straight face.

But this is no laughing matter. Qing-Shen's broadsword gleams razor sharp by his side, and he is not in the mood for jokes.

"I will warn you once again. Stand aside. I have no argument with you. My quarrel is with your master and"—Qing-Shen's eyes search until they rest on me—"and with the one-legged boy."

What have I done? I wonder.

Qing-Shen's voice echoes in my brain: *You dare to take my place. You who do not even have two legs.*

Startled, I lean on my crutch for support.

I am not taking your place, I answer. *I am not worthy to be Sensei's successor, but I am still a better warrior than you. I have one leg, but I stand on it with honor.*

Inside my head, I draw the rice-paper blinds closed. The White Crane doesn't want Qing-Shen there. Only Sensei is welcome. And I can see from his smile that he is listening in.

"I will deal with you next." Qing-Shen spits at my foot. Then he spies Mei. "Why are you standing with these foreigners? You are a disgrace to your family."

"My ancestors are proud," Mei says, staring defiantly. "Unlike yours."

"I see I will need to teach you some respect."

Yoshi's eyes flare. If he was angry before, he's twice as angry now.

"If you are keen to fight against girls, I'm willing to challenge," offers Kyoko, hands on hips. Her message is loud and clear. No respect from her, either.

We don't fear Qing-Shen. Perhaps we should, but we do not.

I hop forward and stand beside Yoshi. Qing-Shen raises his eyebrows. "Tiger-Crane combination. It is a powerful move, but not enough to defeat me."

Qing-Shen pulls a sword from either side of his belt. Two blades shine. One is his Chinese broadsword. I've heard it said it takes one hundred days to master. His other hand wields a long, straight dagger. Even harder to handle.

"Together Yoshi and I are powerful," I say. "But he doesn't need my help to fight you."

I step away. I've made my point, and Yoshi sees what China's Warrior cannot. My spirit remains standing beside my blood brother.

Qing-Shen laughs, twirling his swords menacingly close to my face. "It seems your friend is now a sword short."

Expertly, Mikko tosses his sword to Yoshi. Mikko never lets go of his sword. He's given Yoshi much more than an extra blade. Another spirit stands beside mine.

"That won't do you any good. I hear you don't fight anyway."

"Do you remember nothing I taught you?" Sensei says sadly. "The skilled warrior does not need to fight. He has nothing to prove."

"I remember endless lessons about being prepared." Qing-Shen's eyes narrow. "I paid attention to those, and I know all about this samurai kid. He has much to prove. I doubt he can handle one sword, let alone swing a blade with his left hand."

Qing-Shen might know a lot about us, but he doesn't know everything. Mikko's sword is a rare left-handed sword, especially crafted for him by Master Onaku, the greatest swordsmith in all of Japan. It's dangerous even in an unpracticed hand.

"I'll give you one last chance," Qing-Shen offers. "It is Ki-Yaga I want. Move away. You are NOTHING."

And Sensei was right. NOTHING is standing in Qing-Shen's way after all.

"Are you are afraid to fight me?" Yoshi asks. "I find it hard to believe that China's Warrior prefers to battle frail old men."

Sensei coughs indignantly.

"There is nothing frail about that old wizard," Qing-Shen says. "I've seen him immobilize a man with just one finger."

"Enough," Abbot Lin interrupts as he sweeps into the room, Du Feng by his side. "It is the boy's right to challenge you. He is the Shaolin Tiger."

Qing-Shen hesitates. Recalculating. "That's just a legend. There is no such creature."

"In times of need, the Shaolin White Tiger will rise to protect those its temple has chosen," the abbot says. "You know the words as well as I do."

"Words from a missing book," Qing-Shen jeers. "I don't believe the book even exists. No one has ever seen it."

"We believe what we feel," Abbot Lin says. "Belief is deep inside us."

Deep where the White Crane curls. And I know what it believes. Sensei says we each have a task waiting for us. It is the one he has prepared us for. And this has always been Yoshi's.

"Since when was Ki-Yaga chosen by the temple?" Qing-Shen demands.

The abbot raises his hand. "Since he answered my call."

Qing-Shen is not convinced. "If the boy is the Shaolin Tiger, who speaks for him? What monk recommends him as the temple's champion?"

"I do." Du Feng steps forward.

"Who are you to say?" Qing-Shen demands. "I have seen you practicing in the fields. A no-name monk from the end of the line. The masters ignore you, and even your fellow monks rarely speak to you."

"I am proud to be overlooked. I am pleased to be at the end of the line." Our friend crosses his arms defiantly. "It is the best place to stand. From there I can see everything, and I can easily see what a fool you are."

The abbot lifts both arms. "This boy is the much-esteemed monk Du Feng. He is my most diligent pupil. The masters have been purposely harsh on him, because he is destined for great things. He is my chosen heir."

The look of astonishment on Du Feng's face is hard to translate, but the look on Sensei's face is easy to read. *I told you so.*

Qing-Shen's cheeks flush with anger. "Enough talking. I accept this challenge. I will speak with my swords."

"First, we must set terms," Yoshi insists. "If you lose, you must promise to never threaten my teacher again."

"And if I win?" Qing-Shen asks. "What will you do for me?"

"I will become your servant," Yoshi says. "I will carry your bags and clean your sandals. I will wash your bowls and serve you tea."

Qing-Shen smirks. "I do not want you." He points at me. "I want him to be my servant."

Yoshi looks surprised, but I'm not. I know what Qing-Shen is trying to do. He wants to make sure I never get the chance to ease Sensei's pain. Not even a little. Qing-Shen doesn't want my master and me to fly together. The Eagle won't let the White Crane soar where Eagle wings could not go.

"I agree," I say without hesitation. "I have NOTH-ING to lose. My friend will pluck your feathers."

Inside my head, Sensei applauds loudly.

Qing-Shen raises his sword. Yoshi stands perfectly still. The slow man moves first, to get a head start. Doing NOTHING, Yoshi is already ahead.

At the last moment, he draws, swinging his weapon to meet Qing-Shen's blade. The room vibrates with the clash of steel.

Around me the world shimmers like a hot afternoon.

Yoshi's flying kick sends the broadsword
spinning across the room.

I see the White Tiger leap into the air, claws extended. The Golden Eagle opens its wings and, tail sweeping like a broadsword, launches upward. Tiger growls. Eagle shrieks. Can one room hold such a powerful collision of *ki*?

Suddenly, the spirits are gone.

"Did you see that?" I gasp.

Kyoko shrugs. Mei and Mikko shake their heads.

But Taji nods. "I felt it. The Tiger and the Eagle were here in this room."

Yoshi and Qing-Shen are still exchanging sword strokes. Gradually, Yoshi buckles beneath the barrage of blows. Swordplay is not his greatest skill. With a rush of lightning strikes, Qing-Shen slices Yoshi's robe into ribbons. With another great swipe, the buttons on Yoshi's jacket fly off. Soon he will be wearing not much more than Sensei.

But I'm not worried. Yoshi doesn't practice sword fighting much. He's good at other things. Like strategy. He doesn't need a sword this time. Yoshi's flying kick sends Qing-Shen's broadsword spinning across the room. He tosses both of his swords away, one to Mikko and one to me, knocking the long dagger from Qing-Shen's hand.

"I taught him that," Du Feng says proudly.

Flicking out, Yoshi's foot curls around Qing-Shen's ankle and catches hard. They crash to the ground together.

"I showed him that," says Mei, nudging my foot to remind me of when I was her victim.

Yoshi has the advantage now. A bird on the ground is no match for a cat. They grapple across the floor, arms locked, fingers clenched. Sweat droplets glisten against Qing-Shen's forehead as he struggles.

But Yoshi's face is calm. Smiling like the Tiger that swallowed the Eagle. Or at least that got a good mouthful of feathers. Now it is Yoshi who glitters, the Tiger's bared teeth gleaming as they sink deep into Qing-Shen's ear.

CHAPTER FOURTEEN

勇

ROAR LIKE
A TIGER

The Eagle's screech rips through the room. Cringing, Mei covers her ears. Kyoko grabs my hand. I like that.

"Stop!" Qing-Shen bellows.

Claws clenched, the Tiger holds fast to its victim.

"He's cheating," yells Qing-Shen.

How can it be dishonorable for a tiger to bite and tear? Sensei and Abbot Lin both shake their heads, overruling the accusation. Two sets of wisdom cannot be outweighed by one man, even if he is screaming in pain.

"Do you concede?" the abbot asks.

Yoshi clamps his teeth tighter.

"Yes." China's Warrior spits the word out.

Immediately, Yoshi releases the ear. Qing-Shen rolls away, clutching the side of his head.

"If you ever come near me again, I will bite it off," snarls Yoshi.

Qing-Shen picks up his sword and wipes the blood that has dripped to his neck. He leaps up to the window and pauses in its frame.

"If we meet again, I will scrape *my* talons down *your* face. Next time, the cat will mew for mercy."

Then he's gone.

"Like the wind," says Mikko.

"All hot air," agrees Du Feng, making us laugh.

We try to lift Yoshi, to raise our hero high. But he's much too heavy, and we collapse, laughing even more.

"I am very proud." Sensei places his palm on Yoshi's shoulder. "You found a way to win without harming more than Qing-Shen's ego."

"I knew he would not want his face permanently damaged," Yoshi says. "He is much too vain."

"Now he really will need to cover his head with a bandage." Kyoko has no compassion for Qing-Shen this time.

Grinning, Taji slaps Yoshi on the back. "You were right again. A true samurai doesn't need a sword."

"Not when he has sharp teeth," Sensei says.

Fully dressed, traveling staff in hand, Sensei is ready to leave. Two monks bring our packs, placing them at our master's feet. *Boom. Boom. Boom.* The gong sounds for afternoon practice, but it is not calling to us anymore. Our time is up. We remove the orange robes of Shaolin and place them in a pile in front of Du Feng.

Tears glisten in the corner of our tutor's eyes. Gently, Kyoko reaches up to wipe them away.

"*Chi, jin, yu,* Teacher." Together, we bow our heads and when we look up again, we are all trying not to cry. Too many tears for even Kyoko's fingers to catch. Saying good-bye is the hardest lesson we have had to learn here.

Abbot Lin turns to face Yoshi. "Until you return," he says.

"How do you know Yoshi will come back?" I ask, surprised.

The abbot smiles knowingly. "Yoshi has left me something very important to look after for him."

Our bags are fully packed. I'm sure Yoshi hasn't left anything behind. What could it be? I look at him for a clue but he's not looking at me. He's smiling at Mei. It's not what but who.

"Look." Du Feng points to an arc of color slashing its way across the sky. It splits our world like sun on a sword blade.

"The Dragon smiles on your journey," says the abbot.

"That's a change." Kyoko reluctantly lifts her pack, ready to go.

"All things change." Abbot Lin nods in Taji's direction. "You carry a piece of the Dragon with you."

Finally, the Dragon is on our side. It is Eagles we have to be wary of now.

"Do you want to know what Confucius would say?" Mei asks with a grin.

"Why not?" Mikko grins, too. "As long as I don't have to memorize it."

"Confucius said that as soon as you put one foot in front of the other, things change."

I look down at my one foot. No wonder I find it hard to accept change.

"Are you sure Confucius wasn't a relative of yours?" Taji teases Sensei.

Laughing, our master turns his staff not toward the ocean and the sea voyage back to Japan but northward. We hurry after him, waving to Mei, Du Feng, and Abbot Lin.

"Where are we going, Sensei?" I ask. "Aren't we heading home?"

"I have a desire to see the Great Wall before I die."

"You're not going to die, are you?" asks Kyoko, wide-eyed with alarm.

"Where are we going, Sensei?" I ask.

Sensei tugs at his beard and smiles. "Not until I am ready. And I am not ready yet."

Mikko digs Taji in the ribs. "Sensei takes death very seriously."

"It's because he's extremely old," Taji says, gently teasing our master.

"You should always take death seriously." Sensei raps his traveling staff on the ground. "One day death will turn and look you in the face. No one laughs then."

We do because we're young and have endless years ahead of us.

"But what if you laugh yourself to death?" Mikko splutters, and Kyoko giggles.

She clutches Taji for support. He tips over and knocks me against Yoshi. The weight of all of us is too much for even a Tiger to hold, and we crash onto the ground in a heap.

Now Sensei guffaws, too.

We know there's really no danger in laughing. "Laughter is a great medicine," Sensei taught us, "powerful enough to heal the soul."

As Yoshi helps me up, I can see that his healing is complete.

"Why are we in such a hurry to see a wall?" asks Taji suspiciously.

Our teacher's eyes twinkle. "Perhaps we will learn something there."

"Not more learning." Mikko groans.

I'm not fooled. I know why Sensei wants to see the Great Wall. Resting with his back against the stone bricks, he'll imagine he is leaning against a cherry tree in the *ryu* compound. He wants to sleep and snore. And dream of what he has left to do.

Overhead, an eagle circles. Yoshi throws his head back, and the Shaolin Tiger roars until it seems even the mountains shake their fist at the sky. The eagle wheels away, screeching. Until the next time. I don't trust Qing-Shen at all.

Looking back toward the temple, the White Crane shudders. For one blurry moment, there's nothing but trees. Is it my imagination or a glimpse of things to come?

"Sensei," I whisper.

"Yes, Niya?"

"The temple won't always be there, will it?"

"No. That, too, will pass," Sensei says. "You cannot

fight change. Not even with one of Master Onaku's swords."

"What can we do? We came to help, and we have done nothing."

"Sometimes NOTHING is enough."

But I am not in the mood for Zen wisdom. I am much too sad.

"You said the abbot would give us something to take away. Something to help ensure the temple survives."

Sensei chuckles, but I can't see anything funny.

"What did you spend all your time doing at the White Tiger Temple?" he asks.

"More practice," my friends chorus.

And now I see what he means.

"The abbot never intended to give us a book, a statue, or even a scroll for safekeeping," I say. "We are taking away the Shaolin skills we learned. We will always have a piece of the temple in our hearts."

Sensei smiles. "And what of this treasure you carry? Is it as heavy as you thought it would be?"

I laugh, twirling around as the White Crane dances with me. My heart is feather light.

THE SEVEN VIRTUES OF BUSHIDO

義 勇 仁 礼 真 名誉 忠誠

GI	rectitude
YU	courage
JIN	benevolence
REI	respect
MAKOTO	honesty
MEIYO	honor
CHUSEI	loyalty

USEFUL WORDS

BOKKEN — a wooden practice sword, usually shaped like a *katana*

BOOM — a wooden pole attached to the mast of a boat, supporting the foot of a sail

BROADSWORD — a single-edged long sword, slightly curved, with a broad cutting blade

CHI, JIN, YU — wisdom, benevolence, and courage

CONFUCIUS — a famous Chinese thinker, teacher, and philosopher who lived from 551 to 479 BC

JUNK — a Chinese sailing vessel

KATANA — a long curved sword, traditional weapon of the samurai

RYU — school

SENSEI — teacher

SHAKUHACHI — a bamboo flute

SHURIKEN STAR — a ninja metal throwing weapon in the shape of a star

TENGU — a mountain goblin priest able to change into a black crow

WAKIZASHI — short pointed dagger, traditional weapon of the samurai

ACKNOWLEDGMENTS

I am, as always, grateful to my writing friends who share my joy and frustration when a word falls in or out of the right place. Di Bates, Bill Condon, Vicki Stanton, Mo Johnson, and Sally Hall—thank you. My sons, Jackson and Cassidy, always ensure that I'll have at least two fans.

This book would never have been written without the support (literally!) of my good friends Sharon Hanlon and Barbara Brown, whose shoulders I leaned on when, like Niya, I found myself one-legged and on crutches.

My editor, Sue Whiting, waves her pen, and miraculous transformations take place on my pages. Hitches and glitches just disappear. It's true! Finally, thank you to the wonderful team at Walker Books. There's magic happening there, and I am thrilled to be part of it.